GOOD OFFICES

EVELIO ROSERO

GOOD OFFICES

Translated from the Spanish
by Anne McLean with Anna Milsom

A NEW DIRECTIONS BOOK

Originally published as *Los almuerzos* by Tusquets Editores, Barcelona. This edition is published by arrangement with MacLehose Press, an imprint of Quercus, 21 Bloomsbury Square, London WC1A 2NS.

Manufactured in the United States of America
New Directions Books are printed on acid-free paper.
First published as a New Directions Paperbook (NDP1209) in 2011

Library of Congress Cataloging-in-Publication Data
Rosero Diago, Evelio, 1958–
[Almuerzos. English]
Good offices / Evelio Rosero ; translated from the Spanish by Anne McLean and
    Anna Milsom. —1st American paperback ed.
p. cm.
"Originally published as Los almuerzos by Tusquets Editores, Barcelona. This
    edition is published by arrangement with MacLehose Press."
ISBN 978-0-8112-1930-3 (pbk.: alk. paper)
I. McLean, Anne. II. Milsom, Anna. III. Title.
PQ8180.28.O7A6513 2011
863'.64—dc22

                                    2011012524

10 9 8 7 6 5 4 3 2 1

New Directions Books are published for James Laughlin
by New Directions Publishing Corporation
80 Eighth Avenue, New York, NY 10011

For Róbinson Quintero and Rafael del Castillo

… this side of the head of God,
… in the livid neck of the beast,
in the snout of the soul.

CÉSAR VALLEJO

I

HE HAS A TERRIBLE FEAR of being an animal, especially on Thursdays, at lunchtime. "I have this fear," he says to himself, and glimpses his hump reflected in the window. His eyes wander over his eyes: he does not recognize himself. What an other! he thinks. What an other! And examines his face. "On Thursdays," and then, "this Thursday, especially, when it's the old people's turn." Tuesdays for the blind, Mondays for the whores, Fridays for families, Wednesdays for the street kids, Saturdays and Sundays for God, or so says the priest. "To rest the spirits," the Father asks him — or as good as asks him — to pray and swing the censer. Mass, Mass, Mass. There may be Mass every day — the Word of God — but every weekday lunchtime the parish church becomes a living hell. With midday meals like these, there is no eating in peace. They have their lunches. He has to keep an eye on things, take charge, from the outset. On Thursdays, especially, when he has a terrible fear of being an animal. At 10:00

in the morning, crowds of old people start pouring in from the four corners of the city, Bogotá spitting them out by the dozen. They form an impatient line, leaning against the church wall by the side door that leads to the dining hall and that only opens at 12:00 on the dot, come blazing sun or lashing hail like knife pricks. The old people cannot bear any kind of weather or tolerate the fact that the metal door opens only at midday: the line moans, grumbles, and curses. They are the only ones who forget that their lunch is another of Father Almida's acts of charity. They protest as if outside a restaurant, as if they were paying customers. They act as though they were respected clients and he the maître d', their waiter. "I'll complain to your superior," they yell. "We've come a long way," "I want my soup; it's getting late," "I'm sick," "I'm hungry," "Open up, open up, I'm dying," "Open up, I'm already dead." And they do die, as a matter of fact: eleven old people have died in the three years since they began offering Father Almida's Community Meals. They have died in the line or while eating, and Tancredo's dreadful fear of being an animal redoubles: he has to telephone places where no one ever answers — doctors, police, the institutions and foundations with which the Father has an arrangement to provide support in such cases, worthy and charitable individuals who, if they do answer the telephone, become absent-minded just when they are most needed. "We're on our way," they say. "We'll be there in no time." "Just a minute." But he must wait with the body for hours, in the same hall where the meals are served, he and the corpse similarly inert, each in his chair, the only guests at a table littered with leftovers, a funeral feast which the rest of the old people, despite one of their number having died, carry on eating, even mocking the deceased, helping themselves to the remains of his meal — "It's no use to you now" — and stripping him of a hat, a scarf, a handkerchief or his shoes. Luckily for Tancredo, an old person does not die every Thursday. But this does not diminish his fear of becoming an animal. He is always afraid, he has this terrible fear, especially on Thursdays when the meal is over and he has to clear the hall. "Father Almida will expect you next week," he says, and battle commences. A disconsolate din rattles the table, the plates, the cutlery. They are like stunned children. They implore him as if he were a relative, a memory: they call him extraordinary names, names he will dream of later and be unable to believe are real: *Ehich, Schekinah, Ajin, Haytfadik.* "You can't possibly throw me out," they say. Then the protests begin. Whimpering. Pleading. Whining. "I don't want to leave. Where can I hide?" He must lift them up out of their chairs, all of them lethargic, most of them asleep, their stomachs full of soup and shredded pork: their food is served in the form of mush; they have no teeth, much less false ones, and on top of that they eat so slowly, on purpose, as if they never want to finish. Their meals are eternal. But they do finish, in spite of themselves; they finish and he must rouse them by shouting, round them up like reluctant cattle, even pick them up and carry them bodily from the hall, scare them away by clapping his hands and shoving them out of the church. "We'll call Father Almida," protest the ones who are most awake. "We'll complain." He pushes them out, one after the other, forced to play executioner; the old women try to bite him, hang on his neck, clutch at his hair, beg to see Father Almida, because they are his grandmothers, they say, his aunts, his *mamás*, his friends; they offer to work as servants in the church, as cooks or gardeners or seamstresses; some of them hide under the table, crouching and bristling like fiends, threatening with their fingernails; he has to get down on all fours, hunt them, pursue them, corner them, flush them out. And still his work is not done because even though most of the old people accept that they have to be gone until the following Thursday, there are always two or three dotted about the hall who pretend to be dead, or dying, and some have tricked him; sometimes they manage to confuse him and convince him. "We've died," say the most guileless, giving themselves away. "I'm dead, leave me alone." Others remain stock-still, stretched out on the cold brick floor—a pool of spilled soup and rice—eyes rolled back, limbs stiff. Tancredo puts his ear to their chests; he cannot hear their hearts, it always seems, so he resorts to ruses to unmask them, invoking the patience of Job; he tickles them, their dirty ears, their eyelashes, their stinking armpits and the soles of their feet, which smell a thousand times worse, poking his fingers into ancient shoes brimming with ants, damp with sweat, the leather cracked, the soles worn through by the years, shoes that are never taken off, like their socks—if they have any—and when he manages to reach skin it feels slippery, an icy cold that gives him gooseflesh, and he scratches at it roughly, hurriedly. Only if there is no response does he pinch them, and pinch again, and go on pinching — it is the ultimate test — until they moan, smile, laugh, softly at first, in distress, cry out, then shout, and then: "Leave me in peace, I died already," and they insist: "Don't touch me, I'm dead, I died, can't you see?" and in the end become angry: "You killed me," and insult him: "You damned hunchback bastard," and this is when rage boils up in the pit of his stomach, and he fears becoming an animal and gnashing, biting, finishing off all these skeletons of men and women, who knows if they are children or old people, who knows if they are good or wicked, who knows what they are, but they harbour within them the world's vilest evils. Father Almida says yet again: "Resign yourself, Tancredo," and tells him that nothing is worse than old age, nothing more wretched or pitiable. "It is God's last great test," he says, and that is true, but there is nothing more dreadful than discovering whether they are dead or not, or more terrible than Tancredo's fear of being an animal, because it falls to him to find them out, because he alone has to take charge of their meals, take charge of all the lunches, but most of all the old people's meals, the elderly who become more numerous each time, the insolent old ones who pretend to be dead in order to enter the heaven of the parish church, and they exasperate him, they drive him crazy, they demoralize and crush him, because the worst thing is when an old person really has died and he has had to subject them — or rather, subject himself — to this insane, absurd, unavoidable test of tickling and pinching.

"It is your cross to bear," the Father tells him, "and also your redemption. Resign yourself, Tancredo."

At long last they set off into the streets in different directions, a decimated army, each with his or her bundle, a bag of scraps prudently tucked away, and he doesn't know where they will go, where they will sleep that night or the next, or where they will eat tomorrow— perhaps in another church, he thinks, convincing himself of this in order to soothe his conscience. The shouts and shoves with which he thrust them from the church … others will help them, he thinks, and closes the door, but, as he does so, awaiting him, unwelcome, in the other tiny doorway that leads into the church itself, as if placed there by an invisible hand, lean the scrubbing brushes and the broom, the three pails of water, the cloths and the disinfectant soap, the endless work: the floor and walls must be left spick-and-span, the glass in the only window sparkling; the crucifixes adorning the walls must shine; the enormous, rough rectangular cedar table has to gleam, utterly spotless, as if for the Last Supper; and the chairs for the following day, exactly ninety-nine of them, must be made suitably immaculate and arranged in precise formation. Because tomorrow is Family Friday, the only meal attended by the Father, over which he presides accompanied by his household: the three Lilias, Machado the sacristan, his goddaughter, Sabina Cruz, and he himself, the acolyte, he himself, Tancredo, he himself, the hunchback.

What an other, what an other.

Tancredo averts his examining gaze from the window: forsaken.

Generally, it is 5:00 in the afternoon by the time he finishes clearing up, and only then does one of the Lilias appear in the tiny doorway, carrying his lunch on a heavy tray. He has lunch alone, dishevelled, sweaty from cleaning, smelling of rags, of disinfectant, his head bent over the plate, at times almost fearful. Fearful because sooner or later he raises his head and it seems he is still in the company of all those faces with their toothless, drooling mouths, which open ever wider and swallow him up, one arm after the other, one leg after the other; they gulp down his head at a single go. They do not devour him with their mouths alone: they devour him with their eyes, those eyes, dead eyes. He slams his fist on the table, but they do not disappear. "I am the meals," he cries to himself—"I am the meal, I'm still their meal"—and with a racket like that made by the old people fleeing through the streets he lets out one last rasping sigh. "It is your cross," the Father tells him. "It is your cross." Closing his eyes, Tancredo sees more eyes, those eyes. Then he has a dreadful fear of being an animal, but an animal alone, an animal inside itself, devouring itself from within.

This particular Thursday, however, the presence of another of the Lilias saves him from his fear. It is strange: he has not yet finished his lunch when the Lilia appears on the threshold, her ancient voice full of echoes that whisper damply, urgently: "Father Almida needs you. He is in the office." It is the youngest of the Lilias: shivering with cold, framed in the doorway, she wipes her hands on her apron and sighs deeply. Everything to do with the Father stirs her, even makes her stutter; she is attentive to the point of delirium; her eyes shine as if with fear; behind her small, bent frame Tancredo sees part of the presbytery garden, the willow trees, the great, round, yellow stone fountain, the violet afternoon darkening. "Go right now, I'll look after your lunch," she says, wrapped in her black shawl, and makes for the tray, arms outstretched. "I'll reheat it for you later. You can have it in your room."

It is strange because never before, in three years of Community Meals, has Father Almida ordered them to interrupt Tancredo's lunch, his repose, his rest. The Father's orders concerning this were categorical: "You must not bother Tancredo when he is having his lunch." On one of the Tuesdays for the blind he became upset with the three Lilias because they had begged Tancredo, when he had barely finished his work, to help them in the kitchen: they wanted him to move the refrigerator, they wanted to clean out the coal stove, they wanted help pulling out the four electric cookers so they could sweep behind them and, while they were at it, get rid of a mouse's nest that not one of the presbytery's six cats had been able to reach. "Tancredo can help you in the morning," the Father told them. "Any morning, but not after the Meals. He must have his own lunch, he must rest, and then he has to study before bed." He also told them: "Ask nothing of Tancredo after the Meals, unless he and I agree otherwise."

The three Lilias never asked for Tancredo's help with their chores again, except those they had shared since he was a boy: accompanying them to market every Saturday, carrying the shopping, stacking it in the pantry, checking the cookers, repairing any electrical faults, hammering in or pulling out nails — undemanding domestic tasks. His work, over the last three years since he had finished night school, had revolved exclusively around the Community Meals and his private studies, directed and overseen by Father Almida himself: annotated Bible-reading, learning Latin.

His own work will have to wait now, he supposes, along with his shower and a change of clothes. He will have to go to the office, a sort of study where the Father attends to earthly matters and where he is waiting, wanting to see him — he needs me, Tancredo thinks, as the smallest of the Lilias said urgently.

Reverend Father Juan Pablo Almida was not alone. Seated at the oblong table with him was the sacristan. Pale as a sheet, Sacristan Celeste Machado gazed at the hunchback, astonished, as if he had only just met him. The sacristan was an obscure man, a shadow like the Lilias, and not just because he dressed all in black, but because of his deep reserve, a ring of blackness like a pit. Partially deaf besides, he roamed the place like any other shadow, looming up like the walls. Mute and dark. Stony. His inner gloom could freeze you. His eyes and facial expression screamed hatred and disgust, a secret repugnance that seemed exacerbated by proximity to the Lilias, who fled from him, or the presence of Tancredo, whom he ignored. He conversed — or his harsh voice rang out — solely with the Father or with Sabina, his goddaughter, and only when necessary.

Juan Pablo Almida, robust, exuding strength and health from every pore at sixty years of age — looking more like fifty — was at the head of both the table and the conversation. He had just said something his hunchbacked acolyte could not make out, but which—he sensed—referred to him: they were talking about him. The sacristan continued to examine him as though confronted by some ghastly hallucination. Why so surprised? Tancredo thought. Any self-respecting church needs its hunchback; they should know that better than anyone. Or were they astounded by the vast size of his head, the wisdom in his eyes— as Father Almida, describing him, had once put it—his stature, too tall for a hunchback, the extraordinary musculature God had seen fit to bestow on him, without being asked? Tancredo shrugged, resigned, and decided to let them admire him as much as they wished to for a few seconds. Almida and the sacristan were drinking the hazelnut liqueur that the parish lavished on its most distinguished guests or most unexpected visitors. Father Almida waved Tancredo to a chair on his right. As he sat down, he sensed the current of heat emanating from Sabina Cruz at the far end of the office, bent over the black writing-desk, unobtrusively tapping at the typewriter. She was wearing her blue headscarf; she didn't even turn to look at him.

"My right-hand man has arrived," Father Almida said, without taking his eyes off Tancredo. The sacristan inclined his head briefly, cupping his hand around one ear so as not to miss a word, a characteristic gesture that obliged him to turn his face to one side and stretch out his neck, and, as a result, look at his interlocutors out of the corner of his eye, as if spying on them.

Almida got straight to the point, explaining to the hunchback that our sacristan here was exceedingly interested in knowing more about the Community Meals. Those were his words: *exceedingly interested.*

"Tancredo," Almida said in a confidential tone, "today was the meal for the elderly, was it not? How was attendance? Did many come along?"

"Only three empty seats, Father."

"And there are ninety-nine seats." Almida sipped his drink, visibly satisfied.

The sacristan nodded approvingly. Resting his immense, pale, watery eyes on Tancredo, he forced an incredulous smile.

"Is it always like that, the attendance?" he asked.

His eyes drilled into Tancredo. Scrutinizing not just him, but his reply as well. There was an uncertain silence. It seemed to Tancredo a surprising moment to begin such an interrogation. Besides, he felt worn out, exhausted: after the old people crawling around the hall, over and under the table, bathed in soup, steeped in filth and saliva, like a Roman orgy or a witches' Sabbath, to have to face the sacristan's inquisition infuriated him. Once again he experienced the dreadful fear of being an animal, or the desire to be one, which was worse. He imagined himself dashing that table against the ceiling; kicking over the chairs of the Church's two representatives; tipping out their occupants, pissing on their sacred heads; pursuing Sabina, pulling up her heavy lay sister's skirt, ripping into the apparent innocence of her blouse, buttoned up to the neck, pawing her breasts, pinching her belly button, her thighs, her backside. Truly, he thought, aghast, he needed to confess to the Father about his dreadful fear of being an animal, and the sooner the better. He had to reveal his inner turmoil or he would suffocate. His palms sweaty, his knees knocked together beneath the table.

But Father Juan Pablo Almida urged him on. "Tell us about your experiences, Tancredo, your conclusions. We were talking about the Community Meals while waiting for you to finish your work."

The hunchback turned to the sacristan.

"It depends," he said, with considerable effort. "There are days when attendance is lower. I mean, it varies. This year hasn't been the same as last year. You are aware of this, I think." That was his rather general reply to the question.

The sacristan was not satisfied.

"Bear in mind that I am not well informed," he said. "Does attendance vary according to the day of the week?"

"That's right." Tancredo could not help but agree.

"According to the day of the week, more than anything else." Father Almida's voice, his apparent composure, persuaded Tancredo to divulge his information all at once.

"Yes," he said, "In the case of the elderly, there is almost full attendance. Not so with the street children. Their numbers are going down. Nineteen last time. They complain that the police keep an eye on them here, and in a way they're right ... Last week they caught two of them; perhaps they had charges pending. They didn't even let them finish their lunch ..."

The Father and the sacristan exchanged solemn glances.

"It puts them off coming," Tancredo said. He didn't want to

say anything more, hoping they would free him from the conversation. Let him go to the library, to be alone, far from the dreadful fear of being an animal.

But that is not what happened.

"How old are the street children?" the sacristan asked.

"All different ages," the hunchback answered carelessly. And then: "Well, from four to fifteen."

"Four!" The sacristan was astounded. Raising his head, he contemplated the ceiling as if in prayer. Only after a minute had passed, an almost celestial interlude, did he rouse himself. His blue eyes blinked. His voice sounded concerned. "And the attendance levels of the blind?"

Tancredo would have liked to reply: The same as the attendance levels of the angels. But he stopped himself in time, remaining silent for a few seconds. He thought of the blind, the most delightful of diners, or at least the most peaceful, the most thoughtful and always agreeable — with him and with each other. Unlike the street children, they never griped about the menu, and they accepted the end of every meal with seemly resignation, without protest.

The impatience of Father Almida, who was drumming his fingers on the table, spurred Tancredo on.

"As for the blind," he said, "numbers are stable: thirty or forty every Tuesday."

His listeners' expectant silence convinced him to go on.

"The number of prostitutes is going down," he said. "Six last Monday."

There was another silence. Father Almida's curiosity shifted away from the Meals.

"I was reminding Celeste that you are a secondary-school graduate," he said.

"That's right, Father."

"The parish expects to be paying for his studies in philosophy and theology in the not too distant future," Almida said, without looking at anyone. He had been saying the same thing for the three years they had been offering the Community Meals. The hunchback no longer cared about going to university, but it did irritate him, irredeemably so, that Almida should bring up the plan for him to study philosophy and theology at the slightest opportunity, in front of Celeste Machado.

"Tancredo," Almida asked with evident smugness, "what book are we reading?"

Tancredo felt like a trained beast, on show.

"Augustine's *Confessions*," he replied.

"You mean *Saint* Augustine." The sacristan corrected him immediately. And added, sipping his liqueur: "We must not disregard saintliness in a Doctor of the Church. Inescapable, transcendent saintliness, which makes it all the greater."

"That's true," Tancredo was obliged to concede. "Saint Augustine."

"I simply meant to suggest," Father Almida yielded, "that Tancredo does not neglect his studies, even if they aren't officially recognized by the university."

Once more, the sacristan gave the shadow of a nod, this time somewhat forced and unenthusiastic. Juan Pablo Almida was making the hunchback uncomfortable. He must have some hidden agenda to insist so on Tancredo's education.

"We can speak in Latin, if you wish," Almida said.

The sacristan raised his eyebrows and smiled.

"That will not be necessary," he replied.

Who knows whether he said this to protect the hunchback from such a test. As for Tancredo, he was ready, any time. The long hours spent studying at an arid desk, with no other life to live, had not been in vain.

"We can," Father Almida insisted.

Naturally we can, thought the hunchback. We will prove the existence of God in ten ways. And then — Or ten whacks.

"Of course," the sacristan said. "We do not doubt it, Father, if you say so."

He continued to look fixedly at the hunchback.

"How time flies." Glancing at the clock, Almida seemed to be excusing himself. "There is always so much to do," he said.

"Seven o'clock Mass," the sacristan said.

"There is time." Father Almida consulted his watch as well. "There is time."

It was almost 6:00 in the evening and darkness was falling. Part of the garden could be seen from the office. Like hands, the branches of a willow were waving goodbye. A cat half hid in the stone fountain. The wind, gentle and cold, crept along the walls.

Like the dining hall and the office, the sacristy, connected to a passage leading to the interior of the church, was situated on the ground floor on one side of the garden. Beyond the garden, along a little path intersected by an adobe wall, was the back patio: here were the kitchen, the ironing room, the laundry, the shared bathroom, the three Lilias' bedroom and the hunchback's room, as well as the garage where the Father's old Volkswagen was kept. The bedrooms belonging to the Father, to Sacristan Machado and to his goddaughter, Sabina Cruz—each with its own private bathroom—were on the first floor of the presbytery, overlooking the garden; from the garden you could see their wide oak doors along the passage adorned with flowers and vines, as well as the little library where, along with the books, was the improvised altar of a small black-and-white television, which was switched on only for the news, or when religious festivals or papal messages were broadcast live. Deep stone steps covered with creepers led from the garden to the presbytery's first floor.

The church—its three naves, its bell tower, its chapel dedicated to Saint Gertrude with its oratory and confessional, its lofty vestibule and the cruciform violet stained-glass window presiding over it, its choir stalls and its apse—took up three quarters of the property. Nevertheless, the living space was extensive, and the immense room that had been intended for games—with its six ping-pong tables—and had then been used for the Young Christians' theatrical performances, for the games, raffles, collections and bazaars organized by the elderly ladies of the Neighborhood Civic Association, and for chats between clergy and parishioners, was finally turned into the dining hall for the Community Meals. This was Tancredo's disgrace, or his final destination: with secondary school behind him, he could no longer dream of university.

A bird sang outside, and its song came in like a balm, washing over them. The slender hand of Sabina Cruz, meanwhile, poured more hazelnut liqueur into the gold-rimmed glasses. She served Tancredo too, without a greeting, without a glance. This time she left the bottle on the table.

"Hazelnut liqueur." Father Almida read from the label. Something, a faint irony, seemed to inflect his tone.

"Exquisite," the sacristan said, drinking again. "It is sweet and comforting. Thank you, thank you very much."

His light-colored eyes quickly took in the pale, round face of Sabina Cruz, his goddaughter, much paler than his own: a freckled, immutable face. No expression, no emotion animated it.

"It is sweet," Father Almida conceded, continuing to examine the label. "But it's 25 per cent proof: twice as strong as wine."

God only knew, the hunchback thought, what hidden agenda those two representatives of the Church were pursuing, what their obscure purpose had been for calling him in to enquire about the Meals. A cat regarded them attentively from the very top of the shelves. Everyone in the office seemed to have been waiting for the sacristan's goddaughter to finish replenishing the glasses.

Although not albino, Sabina Cruz's hair and complexion gave the impression that she was. Her skin was so white it seemed pink, and her silvery-blonde hair gave off a sort of dim radiance, the light of an agonizing flame. Slight and fragile in appearance, her head bent, she was even younger than Tancredo, but would soon enough look like one of the Lilias. With that blue scarf on her head, she was a nun without a habit. They waited until she was seated behind the distant writing-desk before resuming their conversation. All the same, it was pointless to pretend that the sacristan's goddaughter was not a participant in it, at least as a witness.

"So," the sacristan continued, and now his ironic eyes bored into the hunchback, "you impart the Word of God to stray sheep by way of the Meals."

He said this as though unable to credit it: a hunchback in the service of God.

"Stray?" Tancredo was astonished. And his astonishment was sincere. His listeners' air of expectancy obliged him to explain. "I would say 'to the hungry sheep'."

He immediately regretted his words, not even entirely agreeing with what he had said. The sacristan instantly turned red. But he recovered quickly.

"That's the trouble," he retorted. "We cannot limit the Meals to just being meals." And then, flapping his long, bony fingers: "Nothing more than meals. Meals upon meals."

He too must have his fears, thought Tancredo. Because the sacristan seemed to be exploding: he even ground his teeth for a second. His eyes brightened, as though he was on the point of tears. He prayed silently, or asked for help. Meanwhile Almida appeared to be ignoring his parlous state. Or pretending to ignore it.

The sacristan drew strength from somewhere, from the cold pouring in from the garden.

"Any meeting with God's people," he said, as if imparting a definitive lesson, the first of many, to Tancredo, "must be taken advantage of in all its dimensions."

Now I get you, the hunchback thought.

"Celeste Machado wishes to assist with the Meals," Almida interrupted, confirming what Tancredo had surmised.

"For example," the sacristan went on intensely, "tell us what today's results were, with the old people. How they expressed their concerns. What you said to them, how they responded."

"We barely speak," Tancredo said. "Speaking to the old people is impossible. You'll see. They just want to eat, and then sleep, stay in the dining hall until the following Thursday. They're worn out. They're old. They do not believe."

"They do not believe?" the sacristan spluttered in exasperation. "He said they do not believe, for God's sake … Did you hear that, Father Almida?" He could not manage another word.

"Yes, they believe, they believe. We are convinced that they do. Nothing is impossible for those who distribute the other bread: the Bread of God, His Hope."

Father Almida had spoken. The sacristan wanted to resume his interrogation, but Almida got in first, interrupting him. "Listen," he said. "Listen to Tancredo. He's been doing this for three years. You can join forces and draw your own conclusions."

"I'm talking about senile men and women," the acolyte said, encouraged, "homeless people with no place to rest their heads. People who roam Bogotá all day. Who sleep in doorways. They do not want to hear Father Almida's messages, messages that, nonetheless, I conscientiously read out to them. They want, quite simply, to have lunch. And to sleep. They pay no heed to anyone. They just want something to eat."

He had gone too far, surely. Father Almida coughed several times, as if he were choking.

"If only," he said finally, with a great deal of effort, "we could set up an old people's home, and a permanent canteen, for all of them. But something is better than nothing. It is our grain of sand. You are my great helpers." He gestured toward Sabina, toward Tancredo. He glanced fleetingly at his watch. He sighed. "These chats are very fruitful, thanks be to God. Tancredo is not entirely wrong about the old people: ill health dogs them; they are capricious. It is different with the blind, with the street children ... But, when all is said and done, the elderly do listen, and they believe. They believe, Tancredo, they do believe. They believe. The proximity of death is a real incentive to belief. Every Meal has its spirit, its time, its guest, and the sacrifice differs. Something happens with a woman who comes on Monday, something else with a woman on Friday; Monday's woman is forsaken, a streetwalker, obliged by necessity to succumb, forced to be a symbol of immorality; Friday's woman is a working mother, a daughter, a sister—in any case, woman at her dignified best, the most beautiful symbol of the family."

An awkward, insurmountable silence reigned. The three men turned toward Sabina Cruz, as if she, a woman after all, were the indirect cause of this moment, this doubt, this sensation.

"Who chose the days?" the sacristan asked at last, directing his question to no one in particular. Then his voice darkened. "This is something that has always intrigued me. Why, for example, is Monday reserved for prostitutes?"

"Nobody chose the days," replied Tancredo, cutting him off. Too late he realized that Almida had intended to reply, that he was still trying to respond. But Tancredo beat him to it. "It is what best suits the diners," he said, "their ... occupations. Monday is a dead day for prostitutes, who generally work from Tuesday to Saturday or Sunday."

"Work?" The sacristan's muffled voice was heard.

The hunchback ignored his intervention.

"According to what one of them told us," he continued. "And, begging God's pardon and all of yours, if there's a Monday for shoemakers, there's also a Monday for whores."

Now Almida really did seem to regret having called Tancredo in. He started hawking again, as though trying to dislodge a fish bone. The sacristan had opened his mouth, but did not speak. A cat miaowed from somewhere. The hunchback smiled to himself. It's strange, he thought, catching himself out, his fear, his anger evaporating as he annoyed the sacristan. Judging by appearances, some of his observations were not to his listeners' liking, though he seemed to have enjoyed making them, choosing them and tossing them into the conversation. His fear was transformed into a morbid pleasure. Awkward once again, the two listeners fidgeted in their chairs.

"Work, you've said they work," the sacristan objected, though not saying anything more.

Tancredo decided to ignore the sacristan, who was thrusting

his face, now flushed, toward him. That prostitutes should work was simply unacceptable.

"And why has their attendance gone down?" the sacristan persisted, exasperated. It was obvious that he somehow blamed the prostitutes' absence on the hunchback's negligence.

"The prostitutes who attend are the older ones," Tancredo explained, no less exasperated. "The ones who live alone and work as they please, depending on their luck. The ones who can arrange things for themselves, you understand, organize their own schedules. They are free, in a manner of speaking. And if by chance a Monday finds them without lunch, then they come along. They're already familiar with the benefits the parish offers. They have a free lunch, that's all."

Tancredo thought Almida was smiling to himself surreptitiously. Was the Father making fun of him, perhaps, of his youth, or did he feel only pity?

Hesitantly, the sacristan asked: "Why don't the young ones come?"

"They're shut in. They have … an employer, their … keeper. Someone who won't let them go out, just like that, to a church. It's not easy. Besides, they don't need lunch."

"But how do they know about these meals?" The sacristan continued his interrogation. Now his tone was irritating the hunchback.

Father Almida hurried to reply.

"Tancredo," he said, "it is Tancredo who is in charge of spreading our invitation by word of mouth among the destitute of Bogotá, who unfortunately seem to make up most of the city's population. You know this, Celeste. Thanks to Tancredo's brave and generous work, we can rely on the street children, the blind, the elderly all coming along ..."

"I would like to help him with this as well," the sacristan said finally. "If I may."

"With the greatest pleasure," Father Almida said. "Your assistance will be invaluable."

"Yes," the sacristan said. "That is where the problem lies: absence ... I mean ... perhaps," and he blushed even more, "it is enthusiasm that is missing from the invitations. I do not see that he is sowing the seed; he is merely casting it on barren ground."

The telephone on the black writing-desk rang. Sabina started to reach for it.

"We'll take it in the sacristy," Almida said, standing up, thus bringing the conversation to a close. "Starting next Monday, Celeste and Tancredo will agree their respective duties."

The telephone rang again. Almida did not bat an eyelid.

"Tancredo," he said, "something important is happening today. I will not be officiating at Mass. Celeste and I have to be elsewhere."

The telephone rang once more. For a fleeting moment, Almida and Machado examined the hunchback icily.

"Another priest will be standing in for me," Almida said. "He will be here shortly. You will give him every assistance." He moved toward the sacristy. The cat followed him.

The sacristan left the room smiling broadly, his pale eyes

looking at no one. "Very well, Monday," he said, "6:00 in the morning." The prospect of the following Monday clearly filled him with enthusiasm, or so the hunchback divined. For the sacristan, it meant the start of a different sort of week. Perhaps he felt it was already Monday, that Monday, his Monday; aglow with anticipation, he rushed out after Almida. Tancredo was left alone in the office, alone or in the company of Sabina Cruz.

Because he was getting ready to leave the office when he heard Sabina's almost inaudible voice call his name. She was still behind the black desk, not looking in his direction. She was holding a stack of white paper. He went over to her. "Here are some leaflets for you to distribute around the neighborhood," Sabina said. They were not leaflets; there was nothing written on the sheets of paper. Sabina's nervous glance, her white lashes tipped with gold, darted toward the door, confirming that she and Tancredo were alone. For the first time she looked into his eyes. Her voice was tinged with reproach and resentment.

"You'll have noticed, will you not," she whispered, "that I'm wearing the blue headscarf today?"

"Yes."

"I wore it last Tuesday too," she said with tremendous effort, "and last Sunday. Didn't you see that I was wearing the blue scarf?"

"Yes," Tancredo replied. "It was blue."

Sabina's extremely white hands suddenly dropped the sheets of paper beside the typewriter.

"So"—she spoke rapidly—"why didn't you come either of those nights? Perhaps you're thinking of not visiting me tonight either? I'm not begging you to visit me, I demand that you do, understand? Haven't you realized that?"

She was suffering, wringing her hands over the stack of paper. They both kept glancing at the door, fearful that Father Almida might enter, or Sacristan Machado.

"Sabina," Tancredo whispered, "I was coming up to see you on Sunday, but I bumped into Almida in the library."

"What time was that?"

He felt that Sabina was interrogating him, just like the sacristan.

"It was late," he sighed. "Three in the morning. I was surprised to find the Father awake at that hour. He was surprised to see me too. I told him I was looking for a book, and ... we ended up working on our Latin until dawn."

"And Tuesday?"

"On Tuesday I was just about to ... and I heard noises coming from Machado's room. He must have been awake."

"What time was that? Three in the morning again?"

"Yes."

"What does it matter if Machado is awake?" Sabina's voice rose involuntarily. "We both know the old devil's as deaf as a post."

"He's deaf, Sabina, but not as a post. And he's not just deaf, he's your godfather, and not just your godfather, but your next-door neighbor ..."

"Oh yes?" Sabina interrupted him. Her voice became hoarse. "So I have a keeper too, like the whores?"

"For God's sake, Sabina. I'm just saying he could hear us at any moment."

"Of course he couldn't." Sabina's expression turned scornful; her fingers crumpled and messed up the stack of paper. Her fury was boundless, but so was her fear. She went on looking alternately at Tancredo and at the door. "That's why I put the mattress on the floor," she said. "So we won't make noise. It's the bed that's noisy, but we don't use the bed. Just the mattress. We don't worry, my God. We never worry."

She stopped, frightened by her own words. She was a little girl explaining the rules of a game. She wore her blue scarf to show, silently, that she wanted to be visited that night. She took a deep breath.

"I want you to come today," she said finally, as if issuing an order. "Today, right?" Her voice cracked. Then, gently, she added, as if pleading with him: "Tancredo, come up tonight, I beg you, for God's sake, I need you." Her trembling fingers grazed the hunchback's fingers. Her yellow eyes looked directly into his. She had half risen in order to murmur this to him, their faces very close. If at that moment Almida or Machado were to come in, thought the hunchback, it would be difficult to explain that nearness, like the imminence of a kiss.

"No," he said, "I'm not coming."

"Why not?" Sabina Cruz burst out, falling back into the chair, defeated. She did not let go of the hunchback's fingers although he remained standing, his back to the door, his body concealing that entwining of hands in case somebody came in. Night settled in the garden. Now Sabina's pale mouth dared to do the worst; brazenly kissing Tancredo's hands. For the first time (the first time with Sabina), the hunchback was overcome by distaste, as if the cold, slippery skin of the old people were still brushing against him. "You must come today," she told him.

"No, Sabina."

"Why not, if I plead with you? Forget the order. I'm begging you."

"I'm not coming. I don't want to."

Sabina's mouth fell open in a silent cry. She let go of his hands. Tancredo closed his eyes.

"I won't be coming any more," he said.

They were interrupted by one of the Lilias bringing in a jug of coffee and a tray of little cups, which she began to arrange too slowly around the oblong table. Sabina Cruz bit her lips. Tancredo silently welcomed the old woman's arrival, which extricated him from that dangerous, absurd conversation.

"Father Almida and my godfather are in the sacristy," Sabina said to the old woman.

"I know," she replied, and went on setting out the cups, spoons, sugar.

"Take them their coffee in the sacristy," Sabina snapped.

"They will be having their coffee here," the old woman responded, "with you, before they go." She gathered up the gold-rimmed glasses, left almost untouched after having been topped up. "It seems you didn't like the hazelnut liqueur," she said, turning to them with a smile. "Such a waste. The cats aren't tempted by hazelnut liqueur. We'll have to keep it for the Meal on Monday. *They* like it."

"Those women?" Sabina asked indignantly, scandalized. "The Father does not allow alcohol to be served at the Meals."

"But this is *licor de santos*," replied the old woman, as if excusing herself. "It wouldn't harm a child. Of course, it's as sweet as poison, but it's always better to share than to waste."

It was a secret to no one that all their leftovers were destined for the Community Meals, including those at which the presbytery cats turned up their noses, the six fat, contented cats. Sabina waited for the old woman to leave the office, but in vain, because there she remained, smiling at them, holding the tray like a shield. Sabina knotted and unknotted her fingers in desperation.

"Tonight," the old woman announced, "this very night, for the first time in all the years I've lived with him, Reverend Father Juan Pablo Almida will not say Mass."

"We know that already," Sabina said.

Almida had never failed in his duty to the Church. Even when he was ill, he would celebrate the Holy Eucharist, keeping to a strict schedule. Tancredo turned to Sabina Cruz, wanting to quiz her about what was going on. But Sabina seemed not to understand anything. Her mind was focused only on her plea, her invitation to him to visit her room that night as on so many others. Sabina was focusing all her powers of reason, Tancredo thought, on that alone. Her understanding, he thought, was like her body:

carnal. Then they heard the voices of the Father and the sacristan in the garden passage; coming from the sacristy, they stopped a moment to finalize details best not resolved in the office with witnesses present. Sabina's eyes showed her anguish, but her words were cold, categorical. She wanted to speak at once, lest her godfather's imminent arrival prevent her from saying anything. Though she did not care about the proximity of the old woman, she nevertheless did not say exactly what she meant: "Tancredo, if you don't come up to collect the leaflets tonight, I shall come down to give them to you myself, in your room."

A dreadful slip, thought the hunchback, to say this in the old woman's presence. And to say it in such a way, like an impassioned threat. Revealing that it was possible that he might go upstairs in the night merely to collect some leaflets, or that she might come down to give them to him — in his room, at night — when such tasks should only be carried out in the Father's office, or maybe in the library, and during the day, for God's sake, during the day. Sabina Cruz had gone mad.

"I will collect the leaflets," Tancredo said, "here, in the office."

Sabina blushed, belatedly repentant. She bit her lips until they bled, but the voices of the Father and the sacristan kept her from reacting to the Lilia's intrusion: she pretended to busy herself with her work, indifferent to the old woman, who went on watching them and smiling, even nodding suspiciously. The voices of the sacristan and the Father came closer, but then stopped again a few steps from the door. The two men did not see the others. Night had completely taken over the garden. The cold slid in. As the old woman was finally leaving, slipping out like a shadow among shadows, Tancredo heard the Father mention Don Justiniano several times. "Don Justiniano," he said, "Don Justiniano will believe us." And then: "Justiniano, Justiniano." Then the sacristan: "Whom are you talking about, Father?" And the Father: "Don Justiniano." And the sacristan: "Ah, an upright man." And the Father: "True. We need not worry." The sacristan's deafness obliged people to raise their voices when speaking to him, so Almida, while supposing he was speaking in confidence, was in fact shouting. "All this will soon be cleared up," he said. "God is everywhere every day." And, as if he had invoked it, rain began to fall. The parish's two highest representatives came into the office at once, and stared at Sabina and Tancredo as if they didn't recognize them.

"You're here," the Father said. "Well, sit down; let's have our coffee. It is time for coffee, the hallowed moment, praise be to God."

"Like a family, just like a family," the sacristan encouraged them, in spite of himself, while taking his seat. His words were not addressed to any of the Lilias, much less to Tancredo. He conscientiously fulfilled all the duties required of his office; he was a diocesan trustee, as well; he assisted the Father at every one of his Masses, acolyte and altar boy at sixty years of age, happily relieving Tancredo of that special office usually held by a child; and, once the sacrament was over, he went from row to row taking the collection, greeting the oldest parishioners, the only ones he recognized, with a respectful nod; he made sure the altar was kept in immaculate order, and took charge of every baptism, confirmation, first Communion, marriage, midnight Mass, funeral Mass, every Mass except for sung Masses, High Masses, for when Don Paco Lucio the organist died, he would let no one else touch the organ; the instrument was shut up for good, just like the music. This did not matter to the Father, but Sabina, the three Lilias and the hunchback missed the music, the canticles, Don Lucio's velvety bass voice, the choirs of nuns whose voices blazed at Easter. But the sacristan was immutable in the face of requests for music, and thus contented himself in his deafness. "Don Paco is present at every Mass," he said, "and his song is heard for eternity." Tancredo has never tried to reason with him; for as long as he can remember, Sacristan Celeste Machado has hated him.

"Tancredo," Father Almida said, pouring a little hazelnut liqueur into his coffee, "have you lost your mind?" He blinked rapidly. Then, though his expression calmed, his voice continued to admonish. "What is the matter with you? What's all this about the old not believing, and not heeding my missives? Who are you to claim such a thing? Do you have telepathic gifts? Can you see inside their heads? What do *you* know? I'm the one who hears their confessions, for God's sake, Tancredo." He took a sip of coffee. He huffed. Now he couldn't help smiling. "Besides," he said provocatively, "if you have important things to say, you must say them in Latin. Why else have we learned it? We are never going to believe you otherwise." He passed a hand over his face, clearly preoccupied. "Well," he sighed, "we'll talk about this tomorrow. I think we need to hear your confession, don't we? And today you will have to assist at Mass. Father Fitzgerald won't be long. He will officiate, and you shall be his acolyte. Just for today."

The sacristan was listening carefully, turning his right ear in Almida's direction, even cupping one of his wrinkled, trembling hands around it.

"One should never refuse the honor of being an acolyte," he said, without addressing Tancredo directly, of course. He spoke angrily, bitterly, his rage barely suppressed.

"He has not refused," the Father said.

Sabina stood up and poured more coffee into Machado's cup. Her hand shook. For a moment Tancredo thought she was going to spill the hot liquid. No doubt she had just understood that Almida and Machado really would be absent from the church, who knew until what time, and that she and he would be alone, after Mass, because he would be serving as acolyte, an office he had not performed in a long time—the last time had been on Easter Sunday when he was just fifteen. Which meant that Sabina and he would end up alone in the presbytery for the first time in ages. This prospect affected her deeply. Flushed, placid, Tancredo watched her pour coffee into all the cups, then return immediately to her chair, as if fleeing. She seemed to be laughing to herself.

"It's fine with me," Tancredo said, ignoring the sacristan in his turn. "I remember all the steps perfectly."

"How could one forget them?" the sacristan asked, continuing to address only the Father. "Even if he were an idiot in addition to what he already is."

"Please, Celeste." The Father pushed his cup away. "Here in the office we are still in God's house, not just in the church. This entire place is God's house, every nook and cranny, every stick of furniture. We are *all* the Church. We cannot use words that do not honor the presence of the Almighty."

He spoke quietly, so of course the sacristan did not hear him; he could not. The Father sometimes spoke this way to his sacristan, with the obvious wish not to be heard, as if on purpose, to express agreement with others without undermining or mocking Machado; he managed things so that Machado did not realize he was taking sides. The sacristan calmly took another sip of coffee.

Tancredo had been an acolyte and altar boy since he was ten years old. He had been relieved of these responsibilities by mutual agreement with the Father. The hunchback offered no resistance, and neither, he thought, did the parishioners. Having become an acolyte out of a sense of obligation, he found pathetic the fear his presence produced in the children (many of whom cried at the sight of him), as well as the cautious mockery of the men and the restrained but evident repugnance felt by the old ladies of the Neighborhood Civic Association. He can find only one appropriate word to describe himself as an altar boy: absurd. More than a hunchback, he supposes, an absurdity—I am, in a word, an absurdity. Not that this stops the sacristan's goddaughter from kissing my hands and begging me to visit her at night. Such are God's ironic designs, an imponderable puzzle, but who am I to question them? I cannot, and do not want to remember myself as an altar boy, another of His designs, because the fears return, and hatred, my hatred, grows, without any particular object.

The sacristan, it seemed, was genuinely worried, as was Almida. Something was tormenting them. Outside, the rain fell harder.

"It is my house too," Almida said suddenly, as if resuming his reflections out loud. Nobody had ever seen him exasperated, so his outburst surprised them all. He not only shouted these words but slammed his hand down on the table: the coffee jug shook, the little cups rattled, the hazelnut liqueur shuddered. The sacristan heard the cry perfectly. "This is my house," the Father went on. "They have nothing to reproach me for. I do as much good as I can; I consecrate my strength to God; I have spent my whole life in His service. Why come to me with such nonsense? We cannot afford to lose Don Justiniano's funding. They have filled his head with lies. Everything he gives us we give to the poor. Charity is at the heart of everything we do. If we lose the funding, we lose the Meals."

"The truth always triumphs," the sacristan said.

"They are fools," the Father replied, "and they are priests, flesh of our flesh, spirit of our spirit, yet nevertheless an emblem of evil. They want to swindle us out of our funding, by God. We won't be the ones to lose out, though. Many of God's children will suffer. Envy in a priest is three times more sinful. May God forgive them, because I curse them."

The sacristan was pained not so much by the Father's words — which he must have heard before — but because he said them in front of Tancredo.

"Father Fitzgerald will be here soon," Machado said. "The bad weather is holding him up. I rang him from the sacristy, spoke to him personally. We could leave now. He did not indicate that there would be any problems."

"How could he," Father Almida countered vehemently, "when I've stood in for him on a thousand and one occasions? This is the first time I've asked a priest to stand in for me at Mass. The first time in forty years. Forty years," he repeated, looking at the clock. It was 6:40. "Well," he said, "my parishioners must be arriving, God bless them. I can't leave without my replacement being here."

"Father Fitzgerald is very punctual," Machado commented.

Tancredo realized that he should go and arrange the sacred utensils on the altar; the sacristan's eyes were urging him on. He felt as if, without looking at him, they were staring and shouting, "To your duties, dimwit!" Then the office telephone rang. Sabina went to answer it. Astounded, they heard her greeting Father Fitzgerald, which meant he was not even on his way. But then they heard her mention Father Ballesteros. It must be that he was going to replace Father Fitzgerald.

"Mother of God," Almida said, "this is unheard of. Don Justiniano leaves for the airport in two hours. We barely have time to get to his house and speak to him." When Sabina had hung up, Almida ordered her to ring Ballesteros. "If they confirm that Father Ballesteros is on his way, we'll leave, but only if they confirm it, Sabina. You must insist they guarantee that Ballesteros is coming to take my place."

"Don Justiniano will wait for us," Machado said.

Almida chose not to favor him with a glance.

"He is a businessman," he said. "I hope his devotion to the parish will allow him to understand our urgency, our explanations."

"He'll wait for as long as he has to."

"Your mouth to God's ear," the Father snapped. His hands met in the air and rubbed together rapidly. He had to speak to Don Justiniano before the businessman left. The parish's principal funding depended on the results of their meeting.

Don Justiniano was their main benefactor. He invariably attended early Mass on Sunday along with his wife and two of his daughters. He didn't inspire the least confidence in either Sabina or Tancredo. Something dark, violent, and complicated lurked within this small man surrounded by watchful bodyguards. Like a human trap, a vast spider's web in which Almida and the sacristan might find themselves struggling like mosquitoes. Every visit from Don Justiniano meant a case full of money, cases which Reverend Juan Pablo Almida and his sacristan, Celeste Machado, hid carefully on the first floor of the presbytery. On one occasion Don Justiniano had agreed to have lunch with the Father in the presbytery dining room; they had dined alone, behind closed doors. The three Lilias had outdone themselves: spicy potato stew, avocados, passion-fruit pudding, flank steak, fruit cocktail, chicken with dried fruit and almonds, saffron rice with parsley, triple dairy flan, melon, soursop sorbet, stewed *curuba* fruit and a creamy cheese with honey that the Lilias called *manna*. But it had all been in vain, because in the end, lunch had been delivered from the kitchens of the Hilton Hotel: American-style fried chicken breasts, pork loin in sherry, eggs à la king, ravioli in sauce, curried rice, and a Normandy pear tart. Father Almida had apologized to the Lilias. "Don Justiniano insisted," he had told them. "We could not convince him otherwise. What could we do, given that it's his charity that enables us to offer up good works to God? Even though I told him myself that he'd enjoy the flavors cooked by the ladies of our parish much more, three pious women who have been with us helping to do God's work for years, three humble and devout cooks a million times better than any French chef, because they cook with love." This was how Father Almida spoke and charmed his helpers, but only when buoyed up by calmness and inner peace. Now they were in the presence of an irascible, shattered priest who frightened them when Sabina announced that Ballesteros was on the line. It appeared that he was not on his way to the church either.

"This cannot be." Almida took the telephone from her. At his side, the almost albino Sabina Cruz resembled a plaster figurine, another of the Lilias. There was a clap of thunder; one flash of lightning after another lit the garden blue.

"Father Ballesteros," Almida began, "this is the first time I have asked another priest for assistance. I have an urgent, unavoidable appointment, for the good of my parish, and they assured me here that you had promised to come. I've stood in for you on three Sundays."

There was an expectant silence. No doubt Ballesteros was excusing himself, but they could not hear him, so Tancredo and the sacristan devoted the silence to ignoring one another. Their gazes clashing when they heard Almida's exasperated voice, they turned to look at him, clutching the receiver like a drowning man.

"But he hasn't shown up either," he was protesting. "Knowing him as I do, it is quite possible that he won't get here until next year, do you hear me?"

Silence again. Then they followed the Father's gaze as it moved to the doorway of the office. On the threshold, alongside one of the Lilias, listening to every word, drenched to the skin, a priest stood waiting. Reverend Father Juan Pablo Almida hung up slowly and sighed.

"Father Matamoros," he said. "A very good evening to you. You're a Godsend."

II

FOR AS LONG AS TANCREDO can remember, that was the night that shed light on all of his nights, a different and devastating night, the beginning or the end of his life, agony or resurrection, God alone knows which. A solemn night, its strangeness and passion surpassed even the first night he and Sabina had at last lain entwined in a shadowy corner of the courtyard after years of innocent play, and sinned hour upon hour until dawn, as if making up for a century of distance.

The bottle of liqueur was still on the table when Almida and Machado ran out to the courtyard, into the rain, to get into the Volkswagen. The three Lilias escorted them, each armed with an umbrella. The parish's two highest representatives seemed to be running away, their heads bent beneath the umbrellas' protective hollows, their bodies mackintoshed and dark, fleeing toward their unfathomable destiny.

Father Matamoros, Almida's unexpected replacement, stood

waiting in the office; as soon as he saw Tancredo returning from the altar, he collapsed into the nearest chair. "This pious throat still has five minutes," he said. "Give me some of that" — pointing to the bottle. "What is it?" he asked. "Ah, hazelnut liqueur. Very sweet." To the amazement of Sabina, who had just come back in, he drank the rest of the bottle — 25 per cent proof, according to Almida's prudent words — from one of the recently used coffee cups: his roguish eyes, deep and black, lit up for a moment. "It's good against the cold," he said, rubbing his wet hands together.

Of indefinable age, Father Matamoros — Reverend Father San José Matamoros del Palacio — was indeed a rare bird in the parish church, gray and featherless, come from heavens knows where. He wore dark clothes and a gray turtleneck sweater instead of a dog collar; his jacket looked borrowed, it was too big for him; his round-toed school shoes, almost black, were scuffed and the soles were gone, the laces white; he wore square glasses, one lens cracked down the middle, one arm mended with a dirty strip of sticking plaster.

The liqueur finished, he ran with Tancredo to the sacristy (the rain was getting worse and pooling in the garden gutters, overflowing across the stone passage), where, out of breath, he inspected his surroundings, especially the pious hangings that adorned the walls. He crossed himself before a Botticelli *Virgin* and seemed to pray with his eyes, awestruck; Tancredo took advantage of the moment to find a towel and dry the priest's face and hair, his dripping hands, his birdlike neck. Matamoros let him do this without taking his eyes off the merciful Madonna of the *Magnificat*. Then he sighed and took another look around him, nodding. He noted, with a certain irony, an ancient black telephone on a little table. He was surprised by this tucked-away telephone corner, where he also glimpsed a plain, empty chair surrounded by a throng of plaster angels, dismayed virgins and saints, a sort of vanquished army with broken noses, missing arms, half their wings gone or stained, white-eyed, their faces scratched, hands broken and fingers cracked, a strange crowd waiting, no doubt, to be taken off to a resuscitating craftsman, or taken away by the dustman. Matamoros smiled to himself. "A phone for calling God," he said. He took a small yellow comb from his pocket and tamed his mass of wayward hair, using as a mirror the enormous gold ciborium which Almida never wanted to use during his Masses, only God knew why. From the same pocket Matamoros drew a bottle of mouthwash, and — to the hunchback's embarrassment — took two or three slugs, which he spat unceremoniously into that same ciborium. "This'll have to be washed," he said, and only then looked at Tancredo, staring like a bird of prey. "You're my acolyte, right?" he asked, giving the other man's hump the inevitable once-over. He smiled without malice. "Put this," he ordered, "on the altar." As he spoke, he handed Tancredo a glittering, beautifully cut glass cruet filled with water. "I mix the wine with this," he said, and then, his eyes on a bronze crucifix, as if offering an explanation to the Almighty: "During Masses I prefer to drink water I've brought myself." Then he allowed himself to be helped into the sacred vestments without taking his blazing eyes from the attentive hunchback, from his looming hump, which Matamoros examined frankly. "Another cathedral," he said, pointing to it.

At the crucial moment of entering the sanctuary, he turned to Tancredo as if he had forgotten something: "I won't be reading the Gospel," he whispered. "You'll be doing that. I assume you know what day we're on." Then he proceeded calmly toward the whiteness of the altar, which seemed to be floating in a mist; he moved wreathed in the candles' perfume, surrounded by the respectful noise of parishioners getting to their feet. He kissed the center of the altar for a long time, down on one knee, his arms spread like wings, his back glowing under the great embroidered gold cross on his chasuble, then straightened up majestically, passing his eyes over the other, beseeching eyes, and began his Mass. A peculiar beginning, Tancredo thought, shuddering, because — after crossing himself and greeting the congregation in the name of the Father, and of the Son, and of the Holy Spirit, and before beginning the Act of Penitence — Matamoros called them not Dear, but Beloved, brethren.

The hunchback paid little attention to the rest of the greeting: just before positioning himself at the side of the altar, he sensed Sabina observing him from the sacristy. She would be waiting for him until Mass ended, and would carry on waiting until Matamoros left. Then she would launch herself at him and have what she wanted unless Tancredo surrounded himself with the pitiful shield of the Lilias.

Father San José's Mass was no ordinary Mass.

To the surprise and delight of the congregation that evening, it turned out to be a sung Mass. Who could have imagined that

Father Matamoros, besides bringing his own water to the altar, would turn out to be a perfect cantor? Beneath the cold vaulted reaches, his voice seemed to come from heaven. He repeated his invitation to repent, singing: *Beloved brethren, to prepare ourselves to celebrate the sacred mysteries, let us call to mind our sins.* It was as if the organ were sounding. Tancredo lifted his gaze to the marble dome as if escaping and saw the host of painted angels flying among the clouds; he saw them return his gaze and still did not know whether to feel terrified or moved. How long it had been, he thought, since Mass had been sung. The purity of the voice was the air they breathed. Nobody understood anything, but the voice sang on. Of course, none of the congregation dared sing their responses, and so, timidly, like lambs, they said the I confess to Almighty God, and to you, my brothers and sisters, that I have greatly sinned in my thoughts and in my words, in what I have done, and in what I have failed to do, and they beat their chests, whispering in unison through my fault, through my fault, through my most grievous fault, and, after the beating of chests, which resounded like an unearthly drum, and marvelling at it in themselves, exultant, as though finally understanding that their own bodies could sound and sing, they carried on asking blessed Mary ever Virgin, all the Angels and Saints, and you, my brothers and sisters, to pray for me to the Lord our God … There was an infinite silence. Father Matamoros concluded by singing Almighty God have mercy on us, forgive us our sins, and bring us to everlasting life, and then, for the first time as a communion, everyone dared respond with a sung *Amen.*

In the front row — because they attended, without fail, every early and evening Mass — were the three Lilias, so different yet so similar, yoked together by the same name since they had entered Father Almida's service, old, dressed in black, their Sunday best, the three of them with neat little trimmed hats, veils and Missals, patent leather shoes, their hands redolent of onions, their breath smelling of various dishes, in their eyes the flames still lingered, the fatigue from mincing meat and garlic, from squeezing lemons, from cooking until all appetite is lost. That night, however, their eyes watered not from onion juice or bruised radishes but from something like a sacred liquor that flooded their ears and touched their souls and in the end made them cry silently. They smiled like a single Lilia. They formed an island among the faithful, who recognized them by their smell and preferred to give up a whole pew just for them, no neighbors beside or behind them, a privilege or a loneliness which the Lilias, in their almost inordinate innocence, understood as deference on the part of the worshippers toward the women who took care of Father Almida, his breakfast, his immaculate soul and his clean shirt.

Sabina too, hidden in the sacristy, threw herself into the unexpected singing for all she was worth. For a few moments of grace, that apparition of a priest made her forget that she and Tancredo would end up alone in the presbytery, without Almida or Machado; she saw Tancredo's burly back, his tapering hump, his raised head, but in the end she did not see him, he did not matter, she simply listened, intoxicated, to Father San José inviting the parishioners to repent. The priest's canticle, which initially almost made them laugh with panic, now made them weep for joy. When they came to the *Kyrie*, the congregation burst out singing to the Lord that he might have mercy, Christ have mercy, Lord have mercy, and felt themselves rising with the *Gloria* up to God in heaven. Machado repeated it, singing alone, and in Latin. They listened to him, rapt: *Glória in excélsis Deo et in terra pax homínibus bonae voluntátis. Laudámus te, benedícimus te, adorámus te, glorificámus te* ... and at the prayer's end, as one, they all sang a fervent *Amen* that caressed the walls, quivering everywhere, from the altar out to the street.

Several passers-by had stopped in their tracks on overhearing this improbable seven o'clock Mass, surely imagining that there must be some venerable mortal remains by the altar, the commemoration of a bishop, at the very least: but there was no corpse in sight, and the Mass was sung. Even without a corpse, the circumstantial parishioners from the street huddled, captivated, in the doorway. Besides, it was raining, and a sung Mass was a good excuse to take shelter.

Tancredo looked up at the church ceiling again, as if seeking to escape. Father San José's Mass, he thought, was a hybrid, a vivisection; he used passages from outdated Masses containing abandoned conventions, splicing them together with others from the contemporary Mass, which he nevertheless dared to sing in Latin. Immediately after the Offertory, before the *Sanctus*, something occurred that Tancredo thought would appal Father Almida, a priest with forty years of experience: Matamoros, standing, his arms outstretched, leaned his head on the altar and immersed himself in the Secret, not, to everyone's surprise, the customary brief prayer, but a good five minutes' worth, which made Tancredo think, astonished, that Father Matamoros might well be dozing.

He was more amazed — this amazement might have extended to the street children and the blind who frequented the Meals, to the elderly and the prostitutes, to the Pope far away — he was dumbfounded, when helping the Father with the sacred vessels and holding out the cruet for him to mix the water with the wine, unstopping the cruet and offering it — snatched away by anxious, demanding, skeletal hands — it turned him to stone in that corner, the most sacred corner of the church, the altar — it made his hair stand on end, it enraged him, to smell, amid the incense, sharp, bitter aniseed, more cutting than cloves or cinnamon, the scent of the countryside, he thought — *aguardiente*, he realized. Yet he saw Matamoros pour more than half of the liquid into the sacred chalice and drink thirstily. This was the Transubstantiation, and Tancredo could not and did not want to believe that *aguardiente* would be used in the transformation of the bread and wine into the Body and Blood of Christ. For the first time in his life, the acolyte, the hunchback, was scandalized. San José Matamoros, he thought, was not only a priest-cantor but one of those they call a mass-and-mealtime priest, a proper little drunk. Then, after the genuflection, he saw Matamoros do something dreadful: he wiped his mouth on the stole. But Tancredo recovered himself. He had known other priestly lapses, either seen them for himself or heard about them. Even priests, he thought, as Almida taught him to think so often, were flesh and blood exposed to sin, men after all, who could tell all their bones, ordinary men who did the impossible: pronounce the word of God, the ancient word.

In any case, Reverend San José redeemed himself. It was unfair to regard him as a simple little priest. There was his sermon, for example. While Tancredo read the Gospel, San José sat and listened from the marble throne with its elaborate gold armrests, to one side of the altar, lolling against the broad, cushioned back, supporting his head with one hand, eyes closed, exactly as if he were asleep. Indeed, after Tancredo finished his reading, three or four endless minutes passed before Matamoros came back to life and approached the pulpit to begin the sermon. A sermon which had little or nothing to do with the Gospel — which Gospel? Matthew, Luke, Mark, John? His reading rent the heavens, but how could it not, Tancredo said to himself, as it was a sung sermon, a Mass risen out of those who had died. An unusual sermon, besides, in its brevity, full of grace, that struck Tancredo more as a sung poem than as a proper sermon, but a prayer after all, he thought, a prayer to brotherly love that pays no heed to race or creed, the only way — still scorned — of entering heaven, proposed by Christ to humankind as if reaching out a helping hand. It was a Mass of Transparency. When they finished saying the Lord's Prayer, the congregation waited expectantly for Matamoros to repeat it, sung, as he had the *Gloria* and the *Credo*, and so it was, for the grace of all: exquisitely sung in Latin, the Our Father, *qui es in caelis: sanctifecétur nomen tuum; advéniat regnum tuum; fiat volúntas tua, sicut in caelo, et in terra* ... raised them up to heaven. They came down to earth with a bump during Communion, however. Father San José approached the line of the waiting faithful and, with the gesture of a worried, flesh-and-blood man, called for the acolyte's help in supporting the golden ciborium containing the radiant Body of Christ. The communicants were alarmed by his trembling hands; more than once, they feared the hosts would slip from his fingers. They chose to attribute the trembling to the same emotion overpowering them: the plenitude of the singing that had made the Mass an apotheosis of peace. They were on the edge of their seats as they waited for him to finish singing the Prayer after Communion, and when the time finally came to respond and take their leave, all sang *Amen* as one. Their hearts were audible.

Exhausted — to an extent Tancredo had never witnessed in a celebrant finishing Mass — Reverend San José Matamoros bestowed his shaky blessing in the name of the Father, and of the Son, and of the Holy Spirit, and repaired to the sacristy, almost dragging himself along, he seemed so worn out. In despair, Tancredo followed him. Now Mass really had finished: now the angels round the vaulted ceiling were merely painted, and their eyes were Sabina's eyes, summoning him: an angel with Sabina's eyes regarded him from every cloud. It was the earthly caress of the flesh that awaited him — hot, moist. From now on the night belonged to Sabina, he thought, but also to him, with his fears, the desolation of the Meals, the identical days he could already see in front of him.

Mass had finished, but the old ladies of the Neighborhood

Civic Association remained rigid in their seats, pillars of the Church, absorbed in mute song, the silence of centuries.

It was as if no one wanted to leave.

The three Lilias were the first to react by running after Matamoros, whom they found already divested of the sacred garments, breathing heavily, seated in the sacristy's only chair next to the telephone, surrounded by angels and saints, mopping his forehead with a towel. They approached him as if they feared he might not be real, as if they did not believe he existed, and gathered around him, cautiously, as they might around an apparition.

In the silence only the rain could be heard, constant, like an affliction, and the hunchback's toings and froings, as he carefully folded the priestly vestments and arranged them one on top of another inside a great wooden chest. The light from a single bulb was insufficient, and night swallowed up the corners of the room; the three Lilias' bodies could not be discerned: vague shapes, they disappeared into the blackness; only their faces hovered, yellow, wrinkled and whiskery, shining as if witnessing wonders.

"God bless you, Father," one of them said finally. "We had not sung in ages."

The words melted into the silence; the rain fell harder.

"One must sing," the Father said. "One must sing."

With difficulty he turned to look at them. Though he was hoarse, he smiled and said, "Well. Singing is tiring. Sometimes singing is tiring."

"It must be, Father, because it shows. Your face shows it, your voice suffered."

It was not clear which of the Lilias had spoken.

"We would like to offer you some refreshment, Father."

And another, correcting her: "Not us, Father. The parish, the joyful hearts who listened to your Mass."

San José Matamoros snorted and shook his head. No one knew what he meant by this. Did the flattery displease him perhaps? He went very still, surrounded by plaster angels: one angel more.

One of the Lilias insisted: "Father, the word of God sings out. But we haven't heard it sung the way you sing it since we were girls."

And another: "Stay with us. Rest. Of course, if you want to sing some more, we'll go on praying …"

And the third: "Until God calls us to Him."

The Father seemed finally to have understood who they were and smiled broadly.

"Please," he said, "what I need now is a glass of wine, just a glass of wine, please."

And, sincerely: "It's freezing."

One of the Lilias dared to make a suggestion: "Wouldn't a little glass of brandy be better?"

And another: "Brandy warms you up more, Father. And helps more with the singing."

San José's face lit up.

The three Lilias seemed about to go and get a glass of brandy, all at the same time. Hesitating, they looked at one another. "Who's going?" one of them asked. In the end they all went, assiduously, as one.

"We don't want to keep you too long, Father. You need to rest." Neither Tancredo nor the priest knew where Sabina had appeared from. Maybe she had sprung, gloomy and sharp like her voice, from among the statues of angels and saints that inhabited that corner of the sacristy. She had taken off the blue headscarf; her disordered ash-blonde hair hid her face. They went on listening to her, not daring to interrupt. "If you want to, you can go. We'll call you a taxi, you won't get wet. We're not going to delay you; nobody wants to put you out."

Sabina's mouth clapped shut. She appeared to regret her words. Outside, in the world, the rain was easing off.

Tancredo finished putting the vestments away. He wanted to be gone from there, but did not know how to take his leave, escape to his room and stretch out on his bed as if he had just died. On the one hand, he knew Matamoros was drunk, or more than drunk: stunned. He might fall over unconscious at any moment, and Tancredo would have to take charge. On the other hand, the proximity of Sabina was causing him to suffer his terrible fears of being an animal, but a free animal, revelling in the flesh. That fear, the most dreadful of his fears, was now far more dreadful than it was during the Meals, when he did battle with the old people pretending to be dead or, worse still, with the ones who actually were.

"In the kitchen," Tancredo said, coming to a decision. "We'll have something to eat in the kitchen, Father. It's warm in there. It won't take long."

"Whatever you wish," Matamoros replied, his manner conciliatory. He was about to say something decisive, but regarded each of them in turn, his hawklike eyes investigating them, disinterring one by one the days of their lives, their memories, exposing them. Sabina could not withstand that stare; she averted her eyes. Now she looked like a little girl who'd been caught out, blushing. To Tancredo she seemed naked, blushing as though they had surprised her naked, just as he had surprised her once, years before, in the shower, stepping in behind her while Reverend Juan Pablo Almida celebrated Mass with Celeste Machado.

Just then, the three Lilias returned, one of them carrying a tray daintily covered with a little cloth, on the tray a gold-rimmed glass, snacks, and a bottle of brandy.

Matamoros, who had been on the point of saying something, stopped himself, all aglow, and opened his arms.

"Please," he said, "I'm not going to drink alone."

The five residents of the presbytery looked at one another, shocked.

"That's right," one of the Lilias said, obligingly. "We'll all have a drink. It's cold."

"I don't drink," another Lilia said, smiling. With her smile, she seemed to be waiting for them to beg her to drink, to have a drink, to beg her just once, no need to insist.

The third Lilia shook her head. "I don't know," she said. Then, by shrugging her shoulders, seemed to say: "Not for me, but you go ahead."

"Me neither," Tancredo said. "No matter, Father. We'll keep you company."

"Father," Sabina said, "we're not allowed to drink. And even if we were, none us who live in the presbytery would want to, not now, not ever. Father Almida very occasionally has a drink from the bottle they've brought you …"

"It's not the same bottle, señorita," one of the Lilias interrupted sweetly, as if explaining the best way to make bread. And she started laughing, softly, generously. "There are lots of these bottles, lots and lots, all the same. Before bed, señorita, Father Almida and your godfather, Sacristan Celeste Machado, always drink a big glass of warm milk with an even bigger glass of brandy. They tell us it helps them to sleep. We believe them."

Sabina flushed.

"Really?" she asked the Lilias, as if threatening them. "Do you also put yourselves to sleep with brandy?"

"Sometimes," replied the Lilia who had previously said, "I don't know." Then she added, thoughtfully: "Although mint tea is better."

Biting her lip, Sabina confronted her. "Reverend Almida will hear about this, you can be sure. We'll see what he makes of it."

Matamoros stood up; he seemed about to take his leave. He buttoned his overly large jacket with its big pockets, where he already had his empty cruet tucked away, and rubbed his hands together. "Its cold," he said and smiled. But smiled to himself, or to no one, as if he were elsewhere, a million light years away, joining a chorus of angels, reminding himself of happy times long ago that concerned him alone; as if he had never been with them, all that time, since arriving at the church in the downpour and celebrating Mass and singing; as if he had heard nothing of the caustic exchange between Sabina and the old women. Straightening his jacket, he turned the collar up over his turtleneck. Now they saw that he was skinny and old and sad, like one of those people who never want to say goodbye yet say it. Sabina sighed: a weight was lifting from her; at last the priest would leave. But Father Matamoros turned calmly toward the Lilia holding the tray and, bowing to her, picked up the glass and bottle, and walked off.

In the doorway he stopped.

"Well," he said, "if I'm going to drink alone, it won't be sitting by myself in that solitary chair, surrounded by saints and archangels, while you stand and watch. Let's go to the table."

And he abandoned the sacristy, heading, it seemed, for the office. As soon as they were alone, the presbytery's five residents recovered themselves.

"This is unacceptable," Sabina said. "Father Almida will be angry, and he will have every right. Who asked you for … refreshments? Is this how we obey the Father the first night he trusts us to be alone, in charge of his church? We should all go to bed. Tomorrow is the Family Meal …"

"Sleep?" one of the Lilias asked maliciously, regarding Sabina out of the corner of her eye. The other two cocked their heads attentively, as though listening to Mass. Sabina stepped back, as if someone were pushing her. Tancredo stepped back too, instinctively, and opened his mouth as though preparing to speak. The Lilias know everything, he realized; they've found us out. And then: they found us out, who knows how long ago? Maybe ever since the first day. For a split second, he was terrified, imagining himself without Father Almida's protection, without the presbytery roof over his head, submerged in the perpetual night that is Bogotá. He regretted his nights with Sabina. Yes. It was possible Almida knew too, even the sacristan. That was why they did not trust him, denying him his university education, restricting him to the drudgery of the Meals. "That's it," he repeated to himself. And he scrutinized the three old women one by one, as if seeing them for the first time. None of them took his examination personally; rather, they seemed to feel a certain pity for him, as though he were only a child, a toy, and not to blame for how he was being played.

"We heard a Mass that deserves our gratitude," one of the Lilias said, or they all said at once, because the voice sounded like a vibrant, sung reproach, drowning out the rain. "It wasn't just any old Mass."

No one knew who was the eldest. Although all three were small, two of them were taller than the third and resembled one another; the third looked like their doll. Over the years, they had acquired the same habits and gestures; it was as though they acted as one, without planning to do so, and as though what one of them said had been thought by the other two, so that what the first began was almost completed by the second, who,

unconsciously, as if sharing bread, left time for the third to finish. Machado had once said that the Lilias were going to die on
the same day, and of the same complaint, and that it was also
possible that they would come back to life at the same time.
Almida did not appreciate the joke: he said that on the day of
the Resurrection there could be neither first nor last. He said the
joy of Resurrection would occur simultaneously, so diverting
the conversation away from the Lilias. He never allowed them
to be made fun of. He respected them for some reason, Tancredo thought, and not just for their cooking. Or was he afraid
of them? Sometimes it was as if Almida fled from them, in the
grip of an inexpressible panic, a presentiment.

"As far as the refreshments are concerned," another of them
said, "it's not our decision. Before he left, Juan Pablo Almida
himself suggested we feed the Father when he finished Mass."

"So feed him and get it over with," Sabina said. "We mustn't
waste any more time."

Tancredo looked fleetingly at the door. He was increasingly
annoyed by Sabina's every word, by her imprudence. If the Lilias knew everything, it was unwise to bait them. As a matter of
fact, one of them answered back: "Waste time, señorita. Time
for what?"

Cornered, Sabina exploded.

"Oh, that's enough," she said. "I won't put up with your whispering and your rudeness any longer. It's terrible listening to
your intrigues, your inventions, your lies, but it's more terrible
listening to you, just your voices, and even worse to know you're

out there, behind our backs, spying. If you want to say something to me, say it now; stop beating about the bush."

"What are you talking about, señorita? I don't understand," a Lilia replied, her tone conciliatory. "What do you want us to say? What do you want to hear?"

And another: "You're not the little Sabinita we once knew. For the past few years you've been an ill-mannered little madam. You don't seem like the sacristan's goddaughter any more. It's as if you've never read the Bible. You make the three of us sad, we who watched you grow from a girl, who were your mothers and grandmothers and friends, your servants."

Sabina tensed up, began stamping her foot, fists clenched, lips pursed. In the light of the single bulb, she was more than golden, suffused with the flames of her hair, with the fiery moon of her troubled face. She could not speak for rage. Tancredo rushed to intervene.

"Prepare the meal," he said again. "I should shut up the church."

"The church." The Lilias were startled. "God's church open, by God. How did you forget the doors of the church, Tancredito? A thief could come in at any moment and …"

"And steal God?" Father Matamoros's voice was heard to ask. They saw him leaning in through the doorway. "Are you going to leave me all alone?" he asked. "They might steal me too. Let's chat for a few minutes in peace; then I'll go. The rain is letting up. You … Tancredito … go and shut those doors. We'll wait for you."

The three Lilias immediately moved toward the Father.

"The food is ready," they explained. "It just needs heating up."

"Come with me," Matamoros replied, allowing them to surround him. Sabina approached them; she wanted to say something, she had to say something, to have the last word. But she didn't know what it was.

Tancredo hurried back to the church. Crossing the empty interior, he made sure there was no one in the naves. He even peeked into the chapel of Saint Gertrude; its blue image, with eyes that seemed to be slipping away as if on a river, held his gaze, and he crossed himself, wanted to say a prayer, but was unsure of which one to say. Still preoccupied, remembering the pungent smell of the *aguardiente* at the altar, he still couldn't believe it; seeming to pray silently, he was thinking of the Inquisition: for that one act alone they might have burned San José Matamoros alive. He imagined the priest on a pyre, in this very church, and smiled: before the fire, the priest would request another *aguardiente*, please. Tancredo smiled more broadly as he checked the confessionals, one by one, in case some thief had taken refuge there. This was not unusual. Thefts from the church were on the rise. Not just valuable objects were stolen, such as the chalice or the linens, but also simple plaster statues, tapers and candlesticks, votive candles, sticks of *palosanto*, censers, collection boxes — one day a prie-dieu, another day a pew, a strip of carpet, even the stone jars in which the holy water was kept, the shabby noticeboard from the entrance, the rubbish bin and, to top it all, the first two steps of the narrow staircase, polished and carved, which in their long ascent spiralling up to the domed ceiling illustrated the Stations of the Cross. However much Reverend Almida publicly exhorted the thief to render unto God the things that are God's, explaining that the staircase had been a present from a Florentine religious society and had, besides, been blessed by Pope Paul VI, the two steps were not returned; worse still, a third and a fourth disappeared, in just three Sundays, and it no longer seemed the work of a thief, but that of a prankster or a fanatic seeking the Pope's blessing. A collector. Bogotá, in any case. Father Almida ordered the rest of the steps to be stored away and replaced with ordinary stairs, made of poor-quality timber, now being eaten away by woodworm.

Tancredo was about to shut the doors when he noticed that the last pew in the church, in the main nave, was completely occupied by motionless women, seven or nine worshippers from the parish, most of them feeble, confused grandmothers, members of the Neighborhood Civic Association. They had been watching him all that time, ever since he had begun to check the confessionals, seek out lurking presences, realign pews, and straighten up the prie-dieux.

"You take a lot of trouble," one of the women said.

Tancredo pretended not to be surprised.

"I have to shut the doors now," he said.

"Doors that ought to remain open," the same woman replied. "But what can we do, Tancredito, if not even God is respected in this country?"

They got to their feet as one and moved toward Tancredo.

"It was a lovely Mass," they said. "For a moment we thought

it wasn't an earthly one. The Reverend who celebrated it must be ... a special person. Thanks to him, we're singing once more. We sing with him and weep for joy. If Doña Cecilia were alive she would have been happy."

And they all made the sign of the cross.

"May she rest in peace," they said in unison. They seemed to go on singing. And moved behind Tancredo to the doors, as if in procession. The rain had eased, but a persistent, stinging drizzle made it even worse out in the street.

"The rain doesn't matter," one of the women said. "It wasn't a waste of a Mass, thank God."

The rest agreed sorrowfully: "Because some are, some are."

They were waiting for Tancredo to say something, but he remained silent.

"We wanted to speak to the Father," they said, letting him off the hook.

"Whenever you like," Tancredo replied. "You can make an appointment, as always."

"You don't understand, Tancredito. We want to speak to the bird who sang before us today. Would that be possible?"

Tancredo had already guessed this.

"Father San José is taking some refreshment," he said.

"So, his name is San José." They were astonished.

"It would have to be, for someone who sings like that."

And then, discussing it among themselves: "Don't disturb him. We'll meet him one day. We need a priest like him so much, don't we?"

"Indeed we do," another replied. "Because, begging God's

pardon, if this priest were in charge of our parish, we'd all be livelier." Having said this, she blushed immediately; none of her companions wanted to, or could, contradict her.

"The Lilias," they said, "our friends the Lilias, the loyal and devoted Lilias, will be able to tell us about Father San José and his whereabouts, with all the details. Don't worry, Tancredito, we'll speak to them."

Satisfied, they began to leave the church, split into groups, arm in arm. They each opened an umbrella; they were like old black birds spreading their wings by the light of the street lamps, in the infinite sparkling refractions of the rain.

"It may only be drizzle, but it's still rain," they said.

Tancredo placed the heavy wooden bars across the door and closed the enormous padlocks. Then, quickly, he crossed back through the church and snuffed out the altar candles, the first thing he ought to have done at the end of Mass; how had he forgotten? He answered his own question: Matamoros, his song, his water. The very presence of that Father in the presbytery was still a latent, unpredictable event. What would happen? Heading for a corner near the altar, Tancredo found—behind an enormous tapestry representing Adam and Eve fleeing the Garden of Eden—the switch that turned off the rest of the electric lights. The darkness swallowed him up completely in the cold of the sanctuary, still redolent of incense, but also of the faint, irritating whiff of *aguardiente*, which caused him to revisit the Mass and hear the priest singing and see him stagger feebly when it came time for Communion. Only the far-off rectangular opening of the sacristy door was dimly illuminated. A slight echo of who knew what voices from who knew where rolled slowly down from the cupola; it was a sound of forsaken souls, a distant sound, but present, as if even at night the church was not empty and other communicants waited, sitting, standing, ailing and healthy, asleep and awake. They were the echoes of the night in the empty church, the nocturnal Mass, Tancredo thought in his distress, when night caught him alone in the church.

Then he felt Sabina's hands in his, hands like startled birds that flew up to his neck and hung on, the cold, swift kiss she pressed on him in desperation. All that time she had been following him.

"Sabina," he said, pulling his face away, "this is the altar."

"The altar," she said, "the altar of my love for you." She seemed maddened from so much love. Speechless, he stumbled, overcome by the strength of the small body, skinny but stubborn, hanging from his neck and, unlike the kiss, burning, shoving him to the marble edge of that same altar, the long, ice-cold table that gleamed upon a base like an upside-down triangle. There they fell, her on top of him, slowly and silently, as Tancredo devoted himself to breaking their fall, and she, voraciously, to kissing him. Suddenly, she took her lips away, exhaled damp breath across the hunchback's face like another well-aimed caress and said: "Don't go or I'll stay under the altar and Father Almida will have to come to get me out and he'll ask me why I'm here and I'll tell him it's because of you, only you." She seemed to be crying as the hunchback lifted her into the air and put her down again to one side, like a wisp; there they sat beneath the marble triangle that Tancredo imagined to be the eye of God, upside down, regarding them. The eye of God, upside down, he thought again, and smiled in spite of himself, adding: What's happening to me? I'm laughing. He remembered smiling recently in church; several times he had smiled right there in the sanctuary; what's happening to me, he wondered again, and tried to see his hands, bewildered, as if they might be wet with blood. At that moment he was not thinking about Sabina at all, only about his hands — they seemed criminal to him — and the eye of God, upside down, spying on them, and then he smiled even more.

"You laugh, you're laughing," Sabina said, and launched herself at him again, trustingly. "This church is like a marketplace," she said. "Those abusive Lilias are taking advantage of Almida's absence. They flounce about like mistresses of the parish, puffed up like turkeys, but lie down like doormats for that little priest to walk all over."

For a moment, Tancredo was overcome by a sort of sympathy and tenderness. There was Sabina, her tempestuous spirit locked inside her fragile blonde body, her reddened lips, pressed together, those teeth that bit them until they bled.

"Let's run away, Tancredo," he heard her say, stunned. "Right now, today, without saying goodbye to anyone. They owe us money, I've got it all planned, I know where to go, where we can live for ever. They won't come after us; why should they? We've worked our whole lives for them. It's only fair we'd get tired of it one day."

He imagined himself running away with Sabina. He could not help smiling again.

She trusted him when he laughed. This time would be no different. She huffed, a flame consuming itself, the only candle still lit. Tancredo sensed her removing her blouse all at once, guessed at the movement in the shadows, the raised arms, the falling garment, utterly overwhelming. As if lit by a black flame, the church grew warm, the air caught fire, smelling of Sabina's pale body, the shiver of her just-uncovered breasts, the sweat in her armpits, and the fear and joy of her ready, daring flesh.

They had been there years before, just once, in the same hollow beneath the altar, children playing with the pleasure of fear, the same fear of being discovered in the church's most sacred corner, the danger of the sacristan appearing, or Father Almida, or the Lilias, the same danger as today, tonight. Tancredo thought: We haven't changed at all, it's the same fear. He smiled again, and once more Sabina was burning above him; it seemed to him that she was exuding smoke, that her flesh must be made of smoldering sticks, of the sweet and bitter smells that enveloped him. But he responded to her kiss—for one instant—more out of pity than desire, then plucked her off him again, like a feather, and said, jumping to his feet: "Cover yourself up," and then, more plea than order: "Come to the office. The Lilias are waiting."

"Never," she replied, retreating and kneeling inside the marble niche. "I'm never going to leave if you don't come here for me, it doesn't matter what time, today or tomorrow or the day after, and I don't care if Father Almida and my godfather or all the men in the world come instead of you, and line up in the church to see me and ask why I'm here, I swear I'll answer them all that it's 'through your fault, through your most grievous fault, Amen,' Tancredo, don't you forget it, I'm never going to leave." The threat came out mixed with sorrow and disappointment.

Tancredo hesitated. About to step through the door into the sacristy, he turned to look back at her, seeking her in the shadows of the altar; he could barely make her out, a quivering smudge; he heard her panting, glimpsed her eyes like blue flames — Tancredo thought he suffered them, two icy, blue hailstones that floated toward him and enveloped him, and felt a confusion of indignant compassion. "We'll be waiting for you," he said again, turning his back on her as if running away, and in reality he did run away, he ran from her, from her threat, a cry laid bare beneath the altar: "I'll be waiting too, my love, I swear I will."

Irritated, Tancredo thought the sacristy smelled of brandy as he passed through it and went out into the garden: he needed to think for a minute, to work things out. It had stopped raining. He tiptoed through the willows. The lit doorway to the office looked yellow. No voices could be heard. Raindrops pattered down from the leaves; they smacked against other big, fallen leaves, against scattered tins which no one ever found; there was the murmur of a drainpipe, gulping water; it was as if it were still raining, without rain. "They're not talking," Tancredo said to himself, "they're not talking" — and he moved closer until he could see into the office. Yellow like the light, the three Lilias seemed to be asleep on their feet around Matamoros, who was seated at the head of the table. In spite of the silence, they were talking; their lips moved; their gestures enquired; their questioning heads responded. Tancredo inched closer. They were whispering. Their voices were like secrets, a confession. As he moved forward slowly, he could make them out.

"So, you're not sisters," Matamoros sighed. His face tilted toward theirs; his hand, meanwhile, went for the bottle at last. He filled his glass, but did not drink. "Not sisters," he repeated. "But you look alike."

"We're from the same village, Father."

"We were neighbors."

The Lilias' voices drifted into the night like stricken murmurings, identical, hurried. They all wanted to talk at once, to say the same things.

"We were cooks, we still are."

"And family? Where are your families?"

"They killed our husbands on the same day in the village. No one knows who did it. One lot said it was the others, the others said it was the first lot. Anyway, they killed all the men. And there were a lot of them. Only we women were left, because they took the children too. We went to ask for them, we looked for them. Imagine, a hoard of mothers asking after a hoard of children. Who knew about them, who had them? One lot said the others, the others said the first lot. Dead or alive, who knows? Thanks to the Lord's infinite mercy we met Father Almida, who had just taken on the church at Ricaurte. We were spared from crying all over the place. We followed the Father from village to village, from city to city. Why would we ever go home again? Our houses were empty, the village would die empty, they weren't there, and they weren't coming back. Without them we were alone, no maize to grind, no homes to keep. But God is great, God is God; Reverend Father Juan Pablo Almida appeared, and for that, God bless Father Almida, although …"

"God bless him," Matamoros said, adding: "I'm not going to drink a toast alone."

They smiled with another murmur. The Father lost patience.

"Go, go and find your glasses and sit with me, and toast with me, before we say our goodbyes. I don't want any food, just a moment with you, to take our minds off the bad weather, and then I'll go. The rain's stopped; God knows when to give and when to take away. I won't need a taxi."

"Don't say that, Father, don't talk of leaving without trying dishes made by no one but us. For the first time in years we cooked because we wanted to, because we really felt like it, and that makes us happy. We're glad to serve you, but it's difficult to sit and have a drink with you. We're not used to that. We just cook, Father, and await the sleep of the just."

As they said this, they moved closer to the priest. The murmuring grew quieter, almost inaudible. The confession.

"But you can't imagine how tired we are of all this, Father."

"That's why I'm telling you to sit down."

"No, Father, don't trouble yourself," one said.

"After all, we're used to being on our feet," another said.

"We suffer from varicose veins, but what can we do?" The third raised her leg with difficulty and unhesitatingly hitched up her skirt to show the Father her calf and most of her thigh, both swollen up like bladders, the branching blue veins, thick and strangling, veins Tancredo already knew about.

"It's tiring work," another said. "Especially the Community Meals. If it were just meals for everyone who lives in the presbytery, fair enough. But the Community Meals are torture. No one shows us any pity, Father. We have to rush from here to there; there are chairs in the kitchen, but we have to walk back and forth constantly, keeping an eye on things. Setting out plates and filling them while the oil bubbles, and careful, the potatoes are burning, while the soup boils, and careful, the potatoes are turning to mush, we have to fly about the whole time, and that's cooking nothing but potatoes, occasionally a bit of pork, who knows what would happen if we were frying cassava and plantain, and the whole time, not a day, not one Sunday set aside by God, not a single morning's rest, because God's children eat every day and we have to prepare their food, it's that simple; if we don't cook, they die. Who knows how many miles we run in a single day?"

The youngest of the Lilias picked up the thread.

"And it's not just varicose veins," she said. "Doing battle with the coal stove, its plates old like us, they get messed up, they come loose, plates that stick out like barbs, sometimes we get burned." And she showed her wrinkled arm, scarred across by a red blister.

It was the night of lamentations, Tancredo thought. A night he too had experienced, in his room, when the three Lilias had come in silently, each with a chair, sat themselves down opposite him and started to describe their tiredness, to show him their burns — couldn't Tancredito speak to the Father and let him know they were ailing, in need of two or three strong girls to help out in the kitchen? They could not do everything on their own.

The wailing had worsened three years back, when the Community Meals had begun; penning the hunchback into any corner, they begged him to intercede with Almida on their behalf; they were dying, they said, sickening in the worst possible way, from fatigue and tedium both. With so many meals to prepare. Even if they were not special meals, just potato soup, creamed potatoes, fried potatoes, stuffed potatoes and mashed potatoes, potatoes in sauce, potatoes in a million and one guises, it was a lot of meals, a vast quantity, too many; they wished they were giants who could dole out potatoes to the whole world, but they were old women, small women, and running around every day is tiring; and besides, they had to take care of the Father's exclusive meals, the sacristan's, their own, also the cats', and all at the same time, every day: either they really were old or from one minute to the next life had become tedious for them. That night Tancredo had paid no attention to their complaints, he'd barely heard them; he'd been astonished to see them seated on the three little chairs around his bed, the three of them wrapped in their black blankets, beneath the moonlight filtering through the window, their faces anxious, afraid, perhaps, of Tancredo himself. "We don't want to believe," they said, "that it's Celeste Machado, God forgive us, who makes Father Almida forget about us." "Why don't you speak to him?" he asked. And they answered: "To the Reverend?" "Yes, to Father Almida." "God bless us, we wouldn't know how, that would be impossible. How could we complain to the person who provides our food and clothing? Maybe he should notice what's wrong himself, but he has his duties too, he's the spiritual leader of this parish, we know his work is unending , how could we ask him to take our needs into account? And yet, when he passes the kitchen and sees us and says hello, he should notice that we've been old for many years already, he should understand we're no longer what we once were and realize that even one sturdy girl would be a help with the heaviest work, the washing-up, for example; we're all arthritic, after the heat of the cookers we can't put our hands into cold water, it hurts our fingers, look, we can hardly bend them; peeling potatoes is pure martyrdom, not because we're lazy, but because we can't stand the pain, it's that simple."

"I'm missing a finger," one of the Lilias dared to say. She had said as much to Tancredo that night, and now repeated it to Matamoros. "It was my own fault. I was chopping onions and trying to remember a dream I'd had that morning. When I was having breakfast I could still remember it, and I felt happy because it was a happy dream, one of those ones that make you laugh to yourself like an idiot, and I wanted to laugh while I was chopping the onions, but I couldn't remember the dream any more … I just couldn't; I think I'd dreamt someone had said two words inside my head, just two wise words I couldn't remember, and trying to remember those two words made me cut off a finger all of a sudden, this one, Father." And she held out one hand; the index finger was missing.

"Of course," Matamoros said, "I cannot see it."

"Don't bother the Father about your finger," another Lilia said.

"Yes," the other said. "You already said it was your fault, so why go on about it?"

"My fault or the dream's fault? I don't know. I mentioned it so the Father understands that our invitation to eat is genuine. If we want to, it's because we want to. For him, we're not tired. For him, I wouldn't mind losing another finger. I'm not just saying it. No one here wants him to leave."

"Samaritan women, meditate on John, chapter 4, verses 7 to 30," the priest said.

"That's it, Father. You won't regret it."

The three Lilias made to leave the office. But all three, possessed and impelled by the same sense, paused unexpectedly in the doorway, putting their hands on their hips at the same time.

"Tancredito," they said into the darkness, "keep the Father company. We'll call you into the kitchen shortly."

All that time they'd known the hunchback was there; all that time they'd guessed he was hidden in the courtyard.

With Tancredo in the office, Matamoros could raise the glass to his lips. Drinking without stopping, he served himself anew. He drank again, more steadily, then filled his glass once more. It seemed as if Tancredo was waiting for him to have a third drink, but Matamoros did not oblige.

"*Nunc dimittis*," he said.

"*Nihil obstat*," Tancredo responded.

There was a silence, then Sabina's voice flooded in.

"You shouldn't be a priest," she said in disgust.

Advancing on Matamoros, she confronted him. There was a great curiosity, too, in her troubled face.

"Why not request dispensation?" she asked. And, eyeing the half-empty bottle, added: "You drink like a laborer. Have you forgotten where we are? Are you that drunk? Is this how you take advantage of Father Almida's trust? I don't mind you taking advantage of the Lilias. I just hope never to see you here again. I wouldn't share a table with you. Tell the Lilias I won't be eating, that I've gone where only God can find me. I'll be waiting there until I die."

"Or until God finds you," Matamoros said, looking at neither of them.

Sabina left as she had arrived, elusive, blazing with rage. Not even glancing at Tancredo, she disappeared into the garden.

"No doubt she's running off to the place where only God can find her," Father Matamoros said. He stood up with the glass in his hand, and, as he drank, leaned out into the night.

"I'd better go," he said.

"Never, Father." The three Lilias had returned.

They took him delicately by the arm. It looked as though they were going to carry him.

"You're coming to the kitchen," they said, "as God meant you to."

And they took him away. Resigned, he let himself be taken.

"Tancredito, bring the bottle," he managed to plead, without turning his head. "Do me that one favor."

III

"THOSE CATS ARE PLAYING TRICKS on us; there are six of them, all from the same family; they used to keep to themselves, but lately they've started bothering us, sneaky, mischievous, obstinate, villainous creatures; there's one, especially, who pees where he shouldn't, shreds the pillows, he's the very devil."

The three Lilias were talking about cats while showing Matamoros around the kitchen: apart from the wedge-shaped pantry and the two refrigerators, there were four insufficient electric cookers, which had to be backed up by a stout, ancient coal stove in one corner: its wrought-iron doors concealed a cavernous oven; its vortex radiated a flickering red atmosphere that was violent rather than warm, a dangerous, menacing fire. Next to this stove the long, rustic table was set under a little window that looked onto the courtyard. In the reddish glow, on the sideboard where pots and pans were hung, in tucked-away nooks, the cats lay curled, grave and furry, watchful, while the Lilias and Matamoros stared at them.

"You can't tell which is the papa and which is the son, but one of them has turned treacherous, and we've found him out. It's that one."

The Lilias were pointing at the same undaunted cat, identical to the rest.

"Are you sure?"

"You can see it in his eyes," they said. The three of them advanced judgementally on the cat. "But this cat's not going to bother us today, are you?" they asked it, wagging threatening fingers, making all sorts of gestures, apparently affectionate, in fact deadly warnings. Then they seemed to forget the cat. Now they were pointing to the table, on which sat a jug of freesias. "Look, Father, for you, a bit of foolishness."

Like strategists directing a battle over unfolded maps, the three Lilias described the dishes, the sweet and the sour, each subtlety and surprise; it was their methodical way of making sense of them: "Follow that with the little bits of orange, Father, to cleanse the palate; munch a slice of apple between cheeses; do try the fish patties, the croissants, the heart-shaped pastries, or that salad with beef and ham in it; look what lovely sausages, the sauce is done to a turn, to a turn, and what's that little rabbit doing there? Waiting for you, Father, and for you, Tancredito; come closer because a meal starts with the eyes; whatever takes your fancy is right here, you just have to reach out a hand and put it in your mouth; let us thank God."

They sat down. "Thank you," the three Lilias said. "Thank you," Tancredo and the priest replied. As if those words had a magical effect, one of the six cats disappeared from its nook, but the Lilias did not take their eyes off it. "We can see you," they said, "we're watching you." The cat, moving in the direction of the table, halted in the Lilias' glare, seemed to change its mind and set off for a better destination: the darkness. Because the light in the kitchen did not reach everywhere. One side of every face consisted of shadows, possibilities. The cat vanished into the blackness, and that worried the Lilias. "We see you," they said, "we're watching you."

But they did not see it, and that tormented them.

"He's the thief," they said, "he likes artichokes, would you believe? He's driving us to despair, he's asking for trouble, as they say; he gives cats a bad name. One day he swallowed the stuffed eggs we'd made for Father Almida, another day the dressed pork medallions. If we're keeping track, we have to count that whole cheese from the coast that he ate all by himself, a month's worth of bacon last March, as well as the fact that he makes our lives a misery, pees on the laundry, hides things, God knows this never happened to us with a cat before, and we've had lots and lots of cats. Benedicto, Calixto, Honorio were the first; they died, then came Aniceto and Seferino; then Simplicio, who lived alone, died, and was replaced by Inocencio, Tera, Bonifacio, and León, Santo, Beato, Félix, Agapito, Justo, Melquíades, Cayo, and Fabiano. Santo was poisoned, Beato and Agapito got run over by a car in the pouring rain, Hilario took their place, then Lucio and Evaristo, Clemente and Sisinio; we've really had lots of cats, Pío, Flamíneo, Triunfo, and Celedonio and a whole lot more names that miaowed, but we never keep female cats, or very few, two or three, they're like some women and only bring suffering, yowling and blood."

"You're very well versed in the names of the Popes," Matamoros said.

"Yes, Father. A way to show our love for the saints and Apostles and God's holy representatives on earth is to give their names to our pets, those we most cherish, with whom we live, eat and wake up; we laugh and cry with them, because they listen, Father, and feel our suffering, they share it; that's why there's nothing sweeter than a little cat called Jesús, for instance, or Simón or Santiago or Pedro, there's nothing like having the Apostles close by, even if they're in the bodies and hearts of cats, but they're God's creatures when all's said and done, are they not? Yet you have to suffer their feline ingratitude from time to time; the one we said is the devil worries us sick, leaves our souls in tatters."

The Lilias scoured the darkness. The cat had very definitely disappeared. They wanted so much to go on talking, but the cat, its absent presence, was upsetting them. And they wanted to talk; how long was it since they had talked? And with a priest, a cantor, so respectful toward them, so attentive.

"Don't worry too much," the Father said. His eyes didn't savor the innumerable treats that brightened the table; rather, they relished the bottles of red wine that accompanied them. Tancredo placed the bottle of brandy at one end of the sideboard, and the Father's eyes followed every move, every detail. He seemed undecided between wine and brandy.

"And that ungrateful cat," he asked, just to say something, so it wouldn't be too obvious that his eyes were pursuing the brandy, "what's he called?"

The three Lilias remained silent. At last, the youngest, flourishing a large piece of bread topped with avocado and prawns, dared to reply: "Almida, Father."

And the others, completely serious, utterly sure of themselves, said: "Yes, Father. He's called Almida. Like Reverend Juan Pablo Almida."

Tancredo's brief, spontaneous guffaw rang out. Neither the Father nor the Lilias took any notice.

"Who would believe it?" Reverend San José Matamoros said. "Almida, the most badly behaved cat of them all."

"The one that does us the most harm."

Again, Tancredo could not contain his laughter.

"What is it, Tancredito?" A Lilia confronted him. "Are we telling jokes?"

Matamoros poured wine into all the glasses.

"There's wine for everyone," he said. And raised his glass to propose a toast. "To Almida," he said. "Not the cat — Reverend Juan Pablo Almida. It is thanks to him that this table is laid."

He blessed the glasses and the three Lilias drank immediately, then came back for more.

It's late, they've been held up — Tancredo was thinking about Almida and the sacristan. Nine o'clock and still not back. Sabina would be beneath the altar, he thought, until God found her, as she said, or as Matamoros said, and as soon as he heard the

Volkswagen's horn he would have to run and warn her, come out, Sabina, Machado's back. Or possibly, disappointed in him, Sabina had gone to bed, plotting for tomorrow, her own accomplice. Anything was possible with Sabina. She might even appear again, utterly exasperated by Matamoros's presence, and not just insult him but might even throw any one of the dishes in his face, or the bottles, or the cookers. After all, it was his stubborn presence that was frustrating her plans: San José Matamoros, the magnificent little Father who was serving more wine to left and right and revelling under the spell of the dishes the Lilias were recommending.

"What do you call that pudding over there?"

"It has no name, Father; everyone calls it something different."

"And that little wing? It looks like a sparrow's."

"Almost, Father. They're from tender little chicks; the meat falls off the bone, try them."

"Is that pineapple?"

"Sugared oranges."

"What a treat, these little strips of crackling on the rice."

"We couldn't fail to include a suckling pig."

"And the wine, saintly women, the wine, by God."

They drank again and Tancredo decided to join in. Although he had not eaten a thing, none of the Lilias thought of encouraging him to do so, as all their attention was focused on the Father, and on the cat too, the vanished cat, who, in a split second, like a lightning flash with phosphorescent eyes, appeared and disappeared, carrying off a drumstick. The three Lilias leapt up from their seats at the same time, with the same shriek.

"There he goes, I saw him, I saw him," they said. "Oh, diabolical Almida! Why didn't you catch him? You were nearest."

They talked among themselves as if weeping and fluttered about out of sight, in despair, at the far end of the kitchen.

"This time he took a drumstick."

"The sly devil."

"And from right under the Father's nose! The shame of it."

"Don't worry about the cat," Matamoros said. "He'll be amusing himself with his chicken."

"How can we not worry? We're just not quick enough," they wailed. "We're not as nimble as we used to be. It's impossible to catch a cat at our age, and Almida, the rascal, is the worst of the lot: he only lets us touch him to stroke him."

"Forget about him."

"And he stole a piece of chicken."

"Don't worry about the chicken."

The three Lilias returned to the table, out of breath. They seized their respective glasses, which Matamoros had topped up again.

"Almida will go on stealing," they said, "and not out of hunger, but to provoke us; after the drumstick, it'll be the wings, and then the rabbit. Father, you'd better hurry or Almida will beat you to it, and goodbye little rabbit, the only one there is, Father, the icing on the cake, that worthy little rabbit."

"I'd rather we talked about the cat, not Reverend Almida." Matamoros's voice was solemn.

"At this hour, one forgets oneself," they said. They licked their lips, stained red by wine. "So much wine in such a short time." They were amazed. "Like holy water. But we should change the thief's name. What shall we call him?"

"*Nobody*," Matamoros said. "*Nobody* is the very origin of names." And for the first time, he burst out laughing, at his ease, while the Lilias drank.

"They're drunk," Tancredo said to himself, unable to believe it, "drunk." During the time he spent imagining Sabina beneath the altar, the three Lilias had drunk enough to become inebriated. He really did hear double meanings in their allusions to the cat and to Father Almida. Reverend San José, on the other hand, seemed extremely lucid now and urged them on, comforted them, but it was useless, because the thieving cat was troubling the Lilias, smashing their little happiness to bits, causing them to withdraw, sorrowfully watchful.

"If it weren't for that cat, we'd be happy," one of them said.

It sounded as if she had cried out that they would be happy without Almida.

A sickly smile of unearthly pleasure, of the joy known only to drunkards, lit up Matamoros's face. He began to speak to the Lilias, to fill their ears with secrets, to question them, to reply himself, to persuade and let himself be persuaded, tasting an occasional mouthful, praising it to the skies. His conversation amazed the Lilias, exalted them utterly, and there was no shortage of toasts, clashing glasses now, sprinkling wine over the fruit.

And then it went dark. The light went out. But they were slow to realize, not so much because the coal stove was still casting its reddish glow as because of the Father's unexpected singing: the song and the darkness both were unexpected. Not even Tancredo paid attention to the absence of light. For some time he had been absorbed in Matamoros's words, above all the most recent ones, when he was explaining that he had always wanted to sing, to be a singer from dawn to dawn, from dusk to dusk, from east to west and north to south, so he said, to set out with his song over his shoulder until the day he died. "I used to sing other songs," he had just finished saying, and that was when the light cut out, just as the song appeared, ringing round the tomb of darkness and reverberating in their hearts. Reverend San José Matamoros del Palacio crooned a bolero, sang it halfway through, then a tango, also, whimsically, half of it, and a folk song and a *cumbia* dance tune and a ballad, and went back to another bolero about when the rain falls all around, "and in a far-off village I will stop my wandering and there I will die," he was singing, the closed-in darkness serving as a background to his voice, repeating it, a strange echo of echoes.

"The light's gone out," came the frightened voice of one of the Lilias at last. Straightaway, they heard her move along one side of the table, carefully, without stumbling, and, illuminated, saw the candle flame painting her wrinkled, shining face red. Lighting another candle, she returned to the table. She sat down, fearful like the other Lilias, looking around her: not a cat in sight. All three of them sighed.

"Sing, Father," they pleaded, like girls in a game. "Sing, whether there's light or not."

The priest's voice had already intoxicated Tancredo. He

dreamt along with the words of each song, the miseries and joys they related. He drank as if sleeping, but was actually swept along in a whirl of his own unfamiliar emotions. He was worried about the absence of light, which always frightened Sabina; if she was still beneath the altar, without the glow from the sacristy, it was possible that she would be terrified; she would scream, her screams might coincide with the arrival of Almida and the sacristan. Sabina had been scared of the dark since she was a little girl. Should he go and look for her? Sometimes power outages lasted all night. It was a joke: the electricity came back on with the light of dawn. Or perhaps he was looking for the perfect excuse to run into Sabina's open arms? No, he told himself, he would not go on with Sabina, and found himself petrified: yes, he desired her; he always had, no two ways about it, protected and hallowed by love — love? Ah, he fantasized, if she were still waiting for him beneath the altar, yes, on the altar or underneath it, under and on all the altars in the world, Sabina, a rare vision in his life, since he'd been a boy, a distant little girl with whom he never held even a minute's conversation in peace, always in despair at the possibility of being surprised by Almida or, even worse, the sacristan, the wicked godfather, with such a shadow hanging over them it was impossible to relax; always in hiding, they greeted each other only in passing, when chance brought them together in one of the church's tucked-away corners, and they touched in the courtyard, in their leafy nests, of late in Sabina's room, with terror for their blanket, like that time at the altar, that other time, when they were children at play, the altar to which they went, terrified to touch each other, even though no one ever thought to spy on them there. He desired Sabina because she intimidated him, unlike other earthier, less celestial women, the whores at the Meals; he had got used to the sight of them, eventually, to the point of ignoring them. Tancredo was surprised to find he was crossing himself, hidden in the half-light. He heard the voices of the Lilias, of Matamoros, and strained to understand them.

"There's no happier pair than a boy and a dog," he heard Matamoros say.

And, much later, pulling him out of his reverie, he heard the voice of a Lilia: "This cat acts like it's out on the streets: open your mouth out there, and they'll snatch your tongue."

As she was saying this, the thieving cat had just appeared and disappeared, now carrying off a great strip of crackling. The Lilias watched the speedy getaway, but this time they did not move from their places. Instead of leaping up, they shook their heads and poured themselves more wine; they might even have smiled.

"One remembers forgotten songs," Father Matamoros said. "I'm remembering one for absent friends. I learned it years ago from the poet Fernando Linero, who played the piano as if he were strumming the clouds."

First he cleared his throat with a good swig; it was the end of the bottle, which one of the Lilias replaced as if by magic, as though not wanting to miss a moment of the song; setting the bottle at the priest's right, she waited as San José burst into song like one more lonely traveler with no place to go, just him and the road, and as he sang his eyes roamed over Tancredo and the Lilias in the candles' flickering gloom. What's that cat doing on the table, so sure of itself? Tancredo fretted for a second—washing its whiskers, listening attentively to Matamoros's song. Now other cats are sauntering across the table, there's one, the epitome of elasticity, wisely settling on the rabbit, unhurriedly finishing off the golden throat, savoring it, spitting out little bones, and no one seems to notice, no one looks at it, the song goes on, the candles crackle as if in response, now the cats even stop eating, seek their lairs with astonishingly calm expressions, set out, reach a corner of the table and leap off one at a time, settle themselves back in their niches, watchful, their eyes fixed on Matamoros's voice, "Dancing," Tancredo said to himself, suddenly noticing the Lilias, "they're dancing"—and so they were. Driven by a lilting waltz Matamoros was whispering, the adoring Lilias were weaving about the kitchen in a silent dance, sunk in a vertigo of the spirits, suspended in the air as if beneath a waterfall, their eyes half-closed, arms raised. Tancredo did not know how much time went by, but suddenly saw that the cats were emerging from their niches again, leaping one by one onto the edge of the table and from there into the darkness; they jumped inordinately slowly, springing lazily into the air, seeming to hang motionless aloft for two or three seconds before disappearing, and at the same time he saw the Lilias were no longer there, it was extraordinary, not a single Lilia seated or dancing around the table. He discovered that Matamoros had stopped singing, but could only shake off the spell of the last song by reaching up and linking his hands behind his head as if stretching. So he was alone with Matamoros; since when? The two of them in the most profound silence; no, Father Matamoros was talking about dreams, telling a dream, or was he singing it? What was Father Matamoros's dream about? How long had he been talking about dreams? Seated at the table, they regarded one another attentively, each on the verge of a word; whose turn was it to speak? Without knowing how, Tancredo resumed the conversation, as if he really had been holding that non-existent conversation with the Father, or did it exist? Whatever the case, he said or carried on saying, as if it were the most natural thing in the world, that he had dreamt, Father, that he had an Indian slave-girl, tied up with a chain like an animal, and that he took her for a walk through a sunlit meadow, the sun, the smell of the sunshine, "everything full of the most terrible lustfulness, Father, hanging over our heads, it was impossible not to take her in my arms, the soft moss offered itself, the leafy oak gave its shade, she stretched out wearily on the grass, it wrapped itself around her like a sheet, offering her rest, and, with the same chain I used for leading her about, she drew me toward her, as if I were the animal and not her, and she spread her legs and all her Hell burned me, Father."

In the silence, one of the candles was dying. Here Matamoros interrupted.

"Why Hell?" he asked.

"Because of the heat."

"The heat, yes, but why Hell?"

"The terrible lustfulness."

"Love, the absence of love."

"Love?"

"Like Joseph in Egypt, I too interpret dreams."

Then Tancredo was not ashamed any more to hear himself telling the Father of his eternal animal fear. I'm telling him of my fear, I should ask him to hear my confession, he thought. "Father, let this be a confession," he said. "God bless you, my child, of what do you accuse yourself?" "Of wanting to kill myself." "In order not to kill someone else?" "In order not to kill someone else, Father." "Speak freely. There exists the secrecy of the confessional, of sinners heard in confession; but in the end God and the dead hear us, see us, they are listening to us." "I don't care if the dead are listening," Tancredo shrugged, his head spinning, "or God." "God doesn't care about that either," Matamoros replied. He seemed to Tancredo to be dozing off; his eyes were closed; he was nodding. Then Tancredo saw him shudder and take a hurried drink. He was reborn.

"What is there to fear?" the priest asked. "There's no sin in wishing to die in order not to kill. These are wearying times, human times. There are good times and bad, and at wearying times the best thing to do is rest."

At last Tancredo was able to make his confession.

"No one can rest here," he said. "We're worked to death."

To tell you the truth, he thought quickly, everyone here wants to kill Almida and his sacristan.

They were talking in whispers, taking frequent drinks, their heads bowed, resting on one hand, their other hands holding the glasses of brandy, while the Lilias remained out of sight. "I'm tired of all this, Father, not because I don't want to do it, but because I can't do it, my head's bursting," something like that. Tancredo shook his head. Was he drunk too? Most likely, because finally he talked about Sabina, his entire life with Sabina, and not just his life, he even revealed where she was at that time of night. "What time is it, Father?" "The time of the heart, my son." Matamoros drank, attentive now. "Where is that furious girl," he asked, "where's she waiting for you?" "You're not going to believe me, Father." "Where, my son?" "At the altar, Father, or, more precisely, beneath the altar; it's her way of telling me she wants me to go away with her; she says if I don't go she'll stay there until Almida comes and finds her."

"Is she capable of that?"

"I don't know."

"Tell me about her."

"It's Sabina's eyes, her tongue wetting her lips when she speaks to me. She convinces me of her schemes, her plotting. It's painful not to give in to what emanates from Sabina's body, her face, all of her, so hopeful of our escape."

Far off but palpable, like vibrations, they heard the voices of the three Lilias, their footsteps in the courtyard. What were they doing out there lost to the world, in the darkness of the immense courtyard, where the Father's Volkswagen would soon be arriving? Tancredo had to hurry; he resumed his confession.

Quite simply, Sabina wanted to be with him, Father, and give free rein to pleasure. Pleasure he was incapable of ignoring; not long ago, while Sabina had been talking to him, he had imagined her naked, and Sabina seemed to discover the desire in his gaze, Father, almost to smell it, because for a few seconds she had stopped talking and even parted her legs slightly, as if making herself comfortable, and smiled imperceptibly, blushing all the more, in anticipation. To roll in each other's arms, oblivious to the world, that was what drove Sabina. To get down to it, and not just beneath the altar, but all over the place, on every altar, wherever, it made no difference, Father. It was her tempestuous spirit locked inside her fragile blonde body, her reddened lips, those teeth that bit them until they bled; it was a different passion, not like resentment or bitterness, that made her suffer and hurt, it was desire, Father, and it all caused him pain, because he desired her too. One day she took him to the little room where Almida and the sacristan keep the money, on the first floor, Father, where no stranger would ever appear, and he allowed her to take his hands in hers and encourage him to follow her. In the library, behind a little door discreetly disguised by three unframed tapestries, they peeked at the boxes of money. There were six rectangular wooden chests, without padlocks, lined up across the secret little room. Around them, stacks of Missals, which the Church printed to give as gifts at First Communions, lined the walls right up to the ceiling. In a corner, piled any which way, lay seven or ten Bibles, dusty and disintegrating, huge, black and forgotten. The six boxes, in contrast, were clean and apparently polished. "Sabina knelt in front of them, Father. She lifted one of the lids: neat bundles of notes filled it up to the top. And she turned to look at me, her hands open on the bundles, messing them up. She ended up sitting on top of the boxes, her chest heaving, her tongue flicking over her lips, moistening them. I didn't recognize her. She crossed her legs and leaned back on her hands. She was looking at me defiantly. 'Let's run away,' she said. 'Any one of these boxes would give us enough to live on. Just one box. I'm not talking about all of them. We've worked our whole lives for these people.' She told me they were mean, that when she'd been a girl they'd never given her a toy, a birthday cake, a decent coat or a scarf, never mind an education, a profession, so that she could be independent. 'What do they want to condemn us to?' she asked, and then supplied the answer: 'To grow old in their service.' She told me her bastard of a godfather, that's how she put it, had taken advantage of her when she was little, not once, but a hundred times. And she struggled not to cry. 'Almida does the same to the factory girls who come to the Community Meals,' she said. That provoked a blind rage in me, Father. The truth is I couldn't refute Sabina's assertions. That has always been my great torment: knowing that she tells the truth. Hearing what she said made me furious, and I wanted to reach out a hand, just my right hand, and wrap my fingers round Sabina's delicate neck, squeeze until it snapped and never hear her again. Why, Father, why that desire of mine to take her life? It was a plan like a cold shudder I didn't know I had in me, but I recognized it the next moment, was amazed by it for an instant, but just an instant, because then I was terrified, Father. Sabina was crying. In any case, with or without tears, it was easy to envisage where she was heading with her words, what her body was hinting at, stretched out beseechingly on top of the boxes, as if pleading that we play an unexpected game. 'Just one box,' she said again, 'and we'll run away.'" As desperate as she was lascivious, she had reached toward him, seized his hands, she was pulling him, her wet lips moving as if in silent prayer. And he saw her naked, suddenly he saw her naked, Father, on top of bundles and bundles of money. Money that didn't belong to her. Money that had begun to pile up at an excessive rate, ever since Don Justiniano had shown up in the parish. And he had preferred not to wonder, never to wonder again, about where that money came from or why it accumulated in boxes, not being deposited in a bank, not being spent, at the very least, on the parish's basic requirements. Well, it was no secret, Father, that the Community Meals were put together at minimum cost, that potato soup and rice with potatoes were the sole insipid ingredients, army mush reserved for the blind, the street children, the prostitutes. With difficulty he pulled away from the hands that were entrapping him, with difficulty, Father, he managed to escape the spell of the body snaking toward him, the burning face on the point of conquering him. And he heard her cry out behind him, Father. "Oh, you great brute," she cried, "coward, a thousand times over," and, in her frustration, Sabina launched herself at the Missals. With a blow she demolished a stack. She tripped over the pile of dusty Bibles. She kicked them. A cloud of dust flew up, sullying the air. "Swine," she cried, "all of you are pigs here."

Silence followed the confession.

"Let's drink," San José said at last, alight. "God has granted us that pleasure."

He got to his feet, coming back to life, and drained his glass. Then he raised one hand as if blessing Tancredo.

"Nothing that has been said here has been proven," he said. "We won't lodge a complaint. Almida and Machado are without stain until God shows us they are not. God is Peace. His Peace proceeds from his presence. In the end, justice will be done, just as He predestines. We have faith in His designs, at least for now."

"For now?" Tancredo said to himself. "What does he mean by 'for now'?"

Complete silence surrounded them. There was no sign of the Lilias in the night. Sabina would still be beneath the altar.

"I'll go to her." The Father heaved a sigh. "To Sabina. I'll take her a glass of wine."

In fact, he already had a glass of wine in his hand. He seized the only burning candle in the other.

Tancredo remained frozen in his seat. He wanted to say something, to warn the Father, but it was impossible. He felt nauseous and, simultaneously, had the urge to laugh.

"I'll go to her," the Father repeated. "No one else must find her beneath the altar; what would her godfather, Celeste Machado, do? He's a bad-tempered man, I know him all too well." He rubbed his exhausted face. "What I'll say to her, I do not know.

I'll sing her that poem by Saint Teresa of Avila." Here Matamoros put his lips close to the hunchback's ear and recited: "Let nothing disturb thee, nothing affright thee, all things are passing, God never changeth, patient endurance attaineth to all things, who God possesseth in nothing is wanting, alone God sufficeth."

When he finished reciting the poem, he began to sing it softly, like a faint peal of laughter, and so left the kitchen, a procession of one, carrying away the light.

Tancredo didn't want to follow the Father, he could not or it did not occur to him; nothing disturbed him, nothing affrighted him, and he drank, God never changed, and he drank again, God alone sufficed. He imagined Sabina confronting Father Matamoros, oh Lord, she would throw the statue of Saint Gertrude in his face, at the very least she would scream, or cry, and he smiled, but what time was it? Midnight? Time, time, time is beyond belief, and Almida not back, where do the cats live, where were the Lilias, where was the world, here, there? In the darkness he scoured the kitchen, feeling his way from memory over every corner, every cooker, every chair; there were no cats, no Lilias, in what other universe would they settle their differences, their mutual vigilance? He remembered them spying on each other: the Lilias on the cats and the cats on the Lilias, a truly unusual enmity, he thought, how had I not noticed it? With that, as if he had invoked it, he heard a distant miaow, like an answer, a miaow that was not characteristic of idleness, of pleasure, but a chilling, blood-curdling miaow. The cats, he thought, the cats are alone, and he went out into the courtyard: the darkness stretched in every direction, the silence, the cold. Then, greeting him, a nascent moon slid from between the storm clouds and colored the corners gray. He heard a splash, the subtle shuddering of water, and in the distance he made out, as though being reborn in the darkness, the three Lilias around the laundry sink, leaning over it, their outstretched arms submerged, but still.

Each was drowning a cat in the freezing water.

From time to time the waters stirred, shuddering, appropriate for death; in the silence little waves rose up, multiplying like storms, because the arms emerged, each pair with their cat, a shadow with paws, panic-stricken, still struggling. The arms plunged them in again, time after time, so slowly, the shadows dripped, defeated, and again the arms and shadows emerged, the shadows not expressing their terror, the arms paralyzed by fatigue, the cats floppy, as if asleep, more dead than alive, but alive, because one of them shook its head, so they submerged them again, until finally hauling them out, stiff as hieroglyphs. "My dear departed," one of the Lilias said, looking around. In the moonlight the other milk-white faces of the Lilias were seeking—what were they seeking? What were they questioning in every corner, in every otherworldly gesture moving things aside, in the wide courtyard gates that opened onto the street, in the garage, in the walls topped by broken bottles, the sharp glass cemented in to cut the hands of thieves, what were they seeking? Their arms let the shadows fall onto the stone surrounding the sink. Their gazes returned to the inner wall separating the court-yard from the garden, the oldest wall, the one made of adobe.

"How are you, Tancredito?" they asked.

They always knew where he was, and when, and why, without needing to see him.

Tancredo's eyes held the most perfect curiosity, but also age-old mistrust; he had endured his own version of the ceremony at the immense stone sink, where once upon a time the Lilias had bathed him and Sabina, naked, as children.

"Why drown them?" he managed to ask, approaching the Lilias.

"How could we not drown them?" they replied, pointing to the six defeated shadows on the edge of the sink. "We warned them ages ago. One of you is asking for it, we told them; you don't let us cook, you drive us to despair with your stealing, we fill your stomachs and you steal, we take away the food and you steal more, what are we to do, cats? Cats like you had never happened to us before, especially you, Almida."

And they pointed at one of the shadows on the stone.

To Tancredo they seemed like strangers. Other women: three demented old ladies from five hundred years ago, alive, but re-constituted from scraps, cobwebs: talking corpses.

"Help us, Tancredito," one of them pleaded with great solemnity. "Help us bury them. They were asking for it. Imagine, one of them ate Father San José's little rabbit, the little rabbit no less. And what time was that, when we didn't notice? At what time did he gobble up that little rabbit that was so good and that we spent so much time over and put so much love and patience into, because we knew it was meant for a saint?"

Another interrupted, whispering: "If he'd only eaten some crackling, big chickens and little ones, every now and again, like he'd been doing before, that would have been fine. But he dared to go for the rabbit, and that was too much. He behaved badly toward us, see. May God forgive us this execution, which is for the good of the parish."

Agile for their years, the three Lilias chose a faraway corner next to the wall, armed themselves with shovels and began to dig. Fascinated, Tancredo observed their work, their despera-tion, their increasing slowness, their clumsy legs, the desolation in their words: "How they've made us suffer," they said, and went back to the task in hand, until they weakened, hands on hips, gray heads directed toward the cats, "How shameful that busi-ness with the priest," they said to them, "aren't you sorry? We'll never forgive ourselves that the little rabbit for him and him alone ended up in one of your stomachs, but which one? The innocent often pay for the guilty, oh wicked devils. Almida, it must have been Almida," they said, "it's this one, he looks alive, it's this one, this one, he laughs, he's laughing."

They suddenly seemed afraid. And, between complaints, dedicated themselves to pummelling the shadowy Almida with their fists. The Lilias' complaints were his own suffering made flesh, Tancredo thought: just like him, a whole lifetime of ser-vice with nothing on the horizon but a whole lifetime of service.

"Father Matamoros is waiting for you," he said.

"No, not yet. We must finish with our hearts what began in

our souls. We already made a start, you saw for yourself. You'd better go, Tancredito, and entertain him. Talk to him about you and Sabina, for example. Why not? His advice will be illuminating. The two of you can't go on as you are, don't you see? One of these days the world will come to an end, and what will we have suffered for?"

That they should call on him to reveal his relationship with Sabina felt like a threat. Tancredo did not know how to reply. Those women knew everything, even from before he was born. He tried to ascertain from the Lilias' faces whether there was mockery or compassion in their words. He discovered nothing there. Unconcerned, they carried on talking as though running through a list, each going in different directions, stopping from time to time at the open grave, staring hard at the cats with wide-open eyes, as if memorizing them, then withdrawing again in one direction or the other, crossing themselves. It was obvious that Tancredo was disturbing them. They were moving impatiently round the courtyard, and now their impatience was not so much to do with burying the cats as with Tancredo leaving the courtyard. Why do I disturb them so? he wondered. Maybe they didn't want to bury their cats, as they should, with him there. Then why ask for his help? Was it possible, he thought, that once he had left the courtyard the Lilias would slither up the walls like giant snakes, roaring with laughter? Would they take to the air, congratulating themselves on their crime? He gave up. Who was he to defend the cats? He went out through the little gate in silence.

Once in the middle of the garden he hesitated. Where to go? He did not want to go near the church or return to the courtyard with the Lilias. A painful fit of laughter doubled him over, choking him. "My God," he said to himself, "how was it they decided to drown the cats? How did they manage to catch them when they all seemed drunk? How were they able they do it?"

He decided to return to the courtyard, groping his way. Taking a deep breath, he leaned over the gate; he could see two of the Lilias dripping in the moonlight: they passed through the night in front of him. The other Lilia, in the depths of the darkness, stomped again and again on the earth bordering the grave. She had still not disposed of her shovel. The others were returning to the sink. "There was a place in the world to bury them after all," one of them said, just as she was passing Tancredo. She stopped suddenly, lit by the moon, stopped in profile, bony, her gray hair falling over her face, her eyes wide, discovering him.

"Tancredito." She raised her voice and smiled as though smiling at a child. "You're not needed here now. Off you go."

And she carried on toward the sink, where the other Lilia was already washing her hands.

Then Tancredo caught sight of the ladies. He caught sight of them just as he turned and left the courtyard. He caught sight of the old ladies of the Neighborhood Civic Association flattened like bats against the walls surrounding the big stone sink. Pale but calm, too serene. How had he not seen them before? They were all there, every one, the same seven or nine devout parishioners, feeble, confused grandmothers who not long ago had said goodnight in the drizzle, at the doors of the church. Seven or nine ladies? At this hour? Celestial grandmothers, housewives, helping to kill cats in the parish church. The whole time Tancredo was in the courtyard they had been hiding, not moving — why? So as not to be seen taking part in such a crime against cats? Surely it went against their dignity. Now, thinking him far away, they came alive again, their sullen expressions came back to life, their murmuring voices revived, they said goodbye furtively, by the light of the moon, and still they carried their umbrellas, in case of rain. They said goodbye to the Lilias, clustered around them. They were whispering. Making suggestions. And they went through the wide courtyard gates in single file, silent as thieves, back to their houses.

As the last one left, Tancredo sought out the Lilias.

"What were the ladies of the Association doing here?" he asked.

The smallest Lilia approached Tancredo and confronted him, eye to eye. Her yellow face was frightening, cold. She shook her head.

"You ask things that you shouldn't," she said.

And with that, still some way off, but coming closer, the sound of the Volkswagen's motor approaching the courtyard gates electrified the Lilias and Tancredo.

"Almida," the women said.

"They're coming," Tancredo said.

He did not run to open up. He could not. He felt thrown into a panic. The world, that night, was too out of kilter. And he admitted to himself, on top of everything, in his heart of hearts, that he had hoped Almida and the sacristan would never come back, that they had disappeared forever, like so many in that country, that the Volkswagen, with no one inside, would end up on some out-of-town rubbish dump, and that Friday's journalists would greet the day with the news: PARISH PRIEST AND SACRIS-TAN DISAPPEAR.

"Tancredito, you go to the office," the Lilias told him. "You should find San José in there. We saw him leave the kitchen. Take care to explain things to him. Pretend the telephone has just rung and you're going to answer it. It's not unusual for us to get up to attend Father Almida, but it's extremely unusual that you and Sabina should be kissing on the altar, isn't it? Off you go now, don't let them see you."

At that moment the courtyard gates opened. The sacristan himself was pushing them, bent and stealthy, in order to let the Volkswagen through, its headlights illuminating strips of shadow.

"The Lilias know everything," Tancredo repeated to himself. The Lilias had spied on them all that time, their whole lives. He and Sabina were never alone. And he fled to the office, as if the telephone really had just rung.

Picking up the receiver, utterly convinced of the telephone's ringing, he heard no voice. Just a continuous buzz that diminished and slipped away into silence. He hung up. If Reverend Almida had come in at that moment, he would have said the telephone had rung. He would have had an excuse for being up, in the office. He would have said that he had been worried by the absence of the Father and the sacristan. He would have concealed the presence of the singing priest there in the church, with Sabina, at the altar. That was the worst, the most inexplicable thing, to explain the presence of Matamoros, drunk, at that hour. But no one came into the office. Tancredo lit a candle on top of the typewriter. He waited a good while, seated near the black writing-desk, contemplating the telephone attentively. How much time had passed? He did not hear Almida's and the sacristan's voices, or their footsteps going up the stairs. Maybe they had already gone up? It was as if two transparent ghosts had arrived instead of the flesh-and-blood Machado and Almida. Without noticing, Tancredo picked up the receiver again and went on studying it attentively. The candle burned low.

"Who was it, Tancredito?" he heard one of the Lilias ask. Who was it, who could it have been, if the telephone had not rung?

Surprised, he noticed one of the old women standing there, the smallest of the Lilias, a shovel still in her hand, sleeves rolled up, arms dirty.

"Nobody," he managed to say.

"And Father San José, Tancredito? I don't see him here. Did he go to the bathroom? Look after him, I beg you. We won't be long. Maybe he left, we'd never forgive ourselves; what would a decent soul be doing out on the streets of Bogotá at this hour?"

"He's in the church," Tancredo said.

"In the church!"

"At the altar."

"Praying, no doubt. What a tremendous priest!"

The Lilia made the sign of the cross.

"Tell him we won't be long. But don't, for God's sake, tell him where we are or what we're doing, for the love of God."

"And Almida?"

"Forget Almida and Machado. They arrived back from Don Justiniano's house with stomach aches. What did they eat? Who knows? What did they give them, what did they stuff them with? Who knows? Perhaps they poisoned them. We've already taken them some mint tea, so they'll sleep like angels." She went out, but came back in immediately and corrected herself: "So they'll sleep, that's all, so they'll sleep like what they are."

The smallest of the Lilias said nothing about the ladies of the Neighborhood Civic Association. She didn't mention them, as if taking for granted that Tancredo had never caught sight of them. But what private talks took place between them, what secrets brought them together in the night, identical in age, in their rapture at San José and his sung Mass? Or were they perhaps a vision? Tancredo shrugged: it was not what mattered to him now.

It was possible that the sound of the Volkswagen, of Almida's and the sacristan's footsteps, had alerted Sabina. How was Sabina? Grabbing another candle, Tancredo made for the sacristy. Going through the church in the gloom, he could not make out the candle San José had taken. Perhaps it had gone out. Besides, he heard no voices. Tancredo raised his own candle to shed a wider light. No one at the altar. Sabina was not there. Then, he thought incredulously, Sabina was vanquished, asleep in her room, or had she gone off to hide somewhere else? In Tancredo's room? And Matamoros? Nowhere to be seen. Tancredo still expected to find Sabina in a far-flung corner of the church, barely reached by the candlelight. It seemed impossible that she was not there. Maybe I want to find her? he thought. Suddenly, the arrival of Almida and the sacristan didn't matter, just Sabina and her body, he thought — Sabina's body and, through her flesh, a sort of freedom.

"Sabina?" he asked the church. His voice bounced back, multiplied, unanswered.

He went up to the altar, to make absolutely sure. He put his candle in a candlestick. Beneath the marble triangle, in the same spot where he had left Sabina, Reverend San José Matamoros was fast asleep. Tancredo lowered the candlelight over the sleeping man: the half-open mouth, a white string of spittle.

"Father," he said.

He saw, beside Matamoros on the marble floor, the priest's glasses, one lens cracked, one arm mended with sticking plaster. His trousers were frayed. One shoe was half off, the sock full of holes.

"Father," he said again, but the priest did not wake up.

"Let him sleep, Tancredito." Once more, the voice of a Lilia chilled him. There they were, their beatific faces leaning over the Father, their hands, this time, empty of cats, shovels, earth, their hands smelling of soap, clasped and held before them as though in prayer.

"Poor thing," they said. "He's fallen asleep. Look at the place he chose. The altar. Where nobody bothers anyone."

Tancredo put the priest's glasses back on his face, passed a hand through his rumpled hair.

"Father."

Matamoros did not wake.

"Let him rest, Tancredito. You'll have to sleep in the sacristy tonight. You should, out of Christian charity, give the Reverend your bed. We'll take him there ourselves."

Sleeping in the sacristy did not alarm Tancredo. On various occasions, due to one of Almida's sisters coming to visit, he'd spent the night there: they had installed a mat for the purpose, a sort of mattress, tucked away among the plaster angels, and, hidden in the mountain of priestly vestments, a pillow and a blanket. It *did* alarm Tancredo that the Lilias should insist on carrying San José's sleeping body themselves.

"Not you, Tancredito. You already helped us enough," they said. Because Tancredo was getting ready to lift Matamoros himself; in fact, he had managed to get his hands under the priest's armpits and was beginning to move him when he felt the bony, vicelike fingers of the Lilias on his arms. There was a short, undeclared battle for the priest's body. With silent force, they obliged Tancredo to lay Matamoros back down on the floor.

"Alright," Tancredo relented. "Very well."

The Lilias' faces were sweating.

"We'll take him there ourselves," they said again. And carefully, with the most exaggerated delicacy, the three raised the priest's body.

"You light the way," they told Tancredo, sarcastically. It

seemed like an order. "At least give us light. Do something, for God's sake.

We do everything around here, all by ourselves, for the love of God."

For a fleeting moment, the Lilias' faces looked demented, unfamiliar. One of them was drooling; the drool dampened her neck, smearing it white, like the froth that spews from the mouths of rabid dogs. The other had popping eyes, and the third displayed a peculiar twisted smile of unhinged happiness on her wide-open mouth, as if about to burst into silent laughter. He did not pay any more attention to them because as he moved out into the garden, beside the Lilias gratefully bearing San José's body, he thought he spotted Sabina. From behind a willow tree, her round, white face peeped out for a moment, or seemed to peep out; it was not her, but the moon, its light uncovered, cloudless; the stars were shimmering in the sky. In the courtyard, where not a single vestige of cats remained, not a shadow, Father Matamoros went on his way in the Lilias' arms, as though he were floating. He was a feather. His face lolled placidly against a skirt; at no time did he stretch or seem as if he might wake up. So still he seemed dead, yet he was snoring, and suddenly snored more and more loudly, out in the air, freely: he was snoring a ludicrous song, another song. Tancredo opened the door to his room, raised the candlestick to light the way and saw how the Lilias lay Matamoros down on the bed, his bed, undressed him with expert care and pulled the covers over him.

"Now go away, Tancredito," they said. "We're going to pray at his side."

"He's asleep."

"But he's snoring, and that's bad."

Tancredo still wanted to find Sabina. It was possible she might be waiting for him in this very room; anything was possible with Sabina. Had they surprised her by arriving unexpectedly with Matamoros? Was she hiding under the bed? Like a children's game, he thought, a shameful game.

"The Father's still asleep," Tancredo said. He hesitated, nothing occurring to him that would provide a pretext for looking for Sabina under the bed. "How can he pray in his sleep?"

"He's snoring, and that's bad. If we pray, he'll stop snoring."

Tancredo knelt and looked under the bed, pulling out slippers he didn't need.

"She's not here," a Lilia said to him. The others were smiling triumphantly and shaking their heads.

"Look for her somewhere else," they said. "Look for her where no one, only God, can find her. We'll see you in the morning."

Another tremendous snore from the Father demanded their attention. Harassed, they turned back to him.

"Like a saint." They began to pray, crossing themselves.

"See you in the morning," they said to Tancredo.

In his corner of the sacristy, lying in total darkness, he expected to encounter Sabina, or that she would appear at his side, stretched out on the mattress with which they were already familiar. Naked beneath the blanket, he believed he was reading the silence, or that the silence was making itself decipherable because it foretold something. He remained alert, peering through the gloom, surrounded by plaster saints and angels, under the little table on which the telephone rested. Was the telephone going to ring, was that the omen? At last he knew that she was present and cried out to himself, "Sabina is finally here." He had a premonition of her, but could not imagine becoming aware of her presence in such a way: she was singing, faintly, but singing, in the church, and she sang as though smiling; her song whimsically crossed the passage that joined the church to the sacristy, it established itself in the gloom, making everything shiver, knocking at the closed church doors, touching the altar, taking flight in the sacred echo of the great painted dome. "Not there, Sabina," Tancredo whispered. The anguish in her voice turned into a laugh in the church, brief but multiplied a hundred times by the echo. "Come and stop me," he heard her say, and the song, like a threat, grew louder. She was singing as though it were a game, a girlish game, but without abandoning the threat, parodying Christmas carols: "Oh come or I shall scream oh come now child divine oh come do not delay." Tancredo sat up, but stayed where he was, hesitant in his nakedness. "Not there," he repeated, "here." Another laugh, bitter, biting, answered him. Then silence. "You come," the voice resumed, urgently, not singing this time. And burst into song again, mockingly: "Let nothing disturb thee, nothing affright thee, all things are passing, God never changeth"—and the voice soared—"patient endurance attaineth to all things." The voice soared, the laughter soared—"Who God possesseth in nothing is wanting"—the voice soared transfigured by the laugh, a laugh that might be colossal, might wake the world—"alone God sufficeth." Tancredo walked in fear and fascination. And went to her, to the place where she said only God could find her. There the heat, the terrifying closeness of the heat of nakedness, the desperation of the kisses he called forth, rushed at him, pulling him out of himself. "God," he cried to himself, and knelt before her, and was thankful for the darkness, because he did not want to see her, or himself.

But he heard her.

"That blessed Father touched my bum," she said, and repeated it in a murmur as if she were singing, happily.

IV

"SEÑORITA, COVER YOUR NAKEDNESS. Look, it's already morning and you've woken up where you shouldn't have done. Aren't you cold? Of course not, you're a little bonfire unto yourself, but what a fire, a wild dog is wet behind the ears compared to you, look at yourself in the mirror: flesh and flesh and flesh."

Sabina came to with a sob and wrapped herself in the blanket. Tancredo barely stirred. The Lilias leaned over them.

"And you, young Tancredo, all the goods out on display? Aren't you embarrassed? We're warning you that in less than twenty minutes Father San José will be celebrating early Friday Mass. Listen, listen, don't you hear footsteps and voices? It's the church waiting to hear the Reverend; the packed church wants to hear him sing, and how's the priest going to sing if he has to come through this sacristy and there are two sinners stretched out beneath the angels? Adam and Eve in the flesh. Ah, God was right to curse them and cast them out of Paradise, because you're just like them, without a single fig leaf, but what are you afraid of? Why the blanket, Sabinita? After all, we know you as God sent you into the world, we used to dress you when you were little, remember? Are you still angry? What were you accusing us of yesterday? Disrespect toward Almida and his church? Ah, God bless them. You'd best go to your rooms and let us tidy up your mess."

"And Almida?" Tancredo managed to ask, still half asleep, rapidly remembering where on earth he was. Slowly, Sabina started to make her escape, wrapped in the blanket, still hating the mocking Lilias, who crossed themselves while watching her, as if they didn't want to forget her.

"Thank the Lord you're not still beneath the altar," they said, crossing themselves, proving that they had spied on the couple the night before. "We've already cleaned and scrubbed," they added, caustically, "and burned all the womanly sweat, all the dirty women's clothing we found beneath the altar, the holy, holy altar."

Stricken, Sabina gave another wail and fled the sacristy.

"What about Machado and Father Almida?" Tancredo insisted. "Aren't they celebrating Mass?"

"They got back in the early hours, remember, and now they're asleep. This morning's Mass will have to be conducted by San José, we think. They looked done in. Oh, Almida and Machado will soon wake up. But by God, it hasn't escaped our notice: this is the very first time they haven't celebrated early Mass. Something good might have happened to them, because we don't want to think it could be something bad. They're asleep. They looked so worn out they couldn't even manage to walk straight. But they got here in the end. Father Almida wasn't about to miss the Family Meal, was he? His favorite day, all those lovely working women who eat like lorry drivers, along with their daughters and granddaughters, all of them flattering Father Almida. What shall we do? Wait. Thank God we have the priest-cantor with us, bless him, whom God helps sing like a bird when it comes to the Mass. We've already served him a good meaty broth, which he diluted with a bottle of wine, more like wine broth, a reviving miracle, because he's like a bee buzzing around a garden now. Come along, Tancredito, and have breakfast, because by the look of you, you didn't sleep well either, you've got circles under your eyes like wells. Are there really no other women in the world for you? More beautiful, purer?"

They're still drunk, Tancredo thought. And, looking at them, he remembered the cats. He found the absence of miaowing strange, had a premonition of the cats' phosphorescent eyes wandering like lost souls all over the presbytery. It seemed like a bad dream that the Lilias had executed them in the laundry sink, encouraged and shielded by the other women, the unfading grandmothers of the Neighborhood Civic Association. They really were that tired of the cats, he thought, unable to suppress a nagging fear of the Lilias' deferential faces. They carried on looking at him attentively. Naked, he still lay on the mattress, one hand raised as though he were physically protecting himself from their words. One of them had seized his clothes and held them under her arm, as if thinking of never returning them. Tancredo reached up, demanding them, and they all burst out laughing.

"Now he wants to get dressed," they said. "About time too."

In the end, the Lilia gave him back his clothes, and he had no option but to get dressed in front of them.

"If we overlook the hump," they said, "your parents were inspired, Tancredito; you look to be well formed, you should thank God."

And they cackled like lunatics while continuing to put the place in order. Only the ringing of the telephone brought them to a standstill.

"Who can that be?" they asked as one, and stared at the telephone, open-mouthed, hands outstretched. It was as if the instrument had Reverend Almida's voice, turning up suddenly in the morning, greeting them all, asking what was going on, questioning them closely about their duties.

Tancredo answered, and, once again, as the night before, there was a continuous buzzing sound which tailed off and died. He hung up, and he and the Lilias stared at the instrument.

"Nobody," he said.

"*Nobody* is the cat that died last night," the smallest Lilia replied, a hint of menace in her voice. The others took advantage of the moment to finish hiding away the mattress, blanket, and pillow. Then they fled, literally, from the sacristy.

"I do hope San José manages to sing," the youngest, the last to leave, was saying when the telephone rang again. Tancredo let it ring twice before answering it. No buzzing, no voice. He hung up. It rang. Tancredo was asking who it was, whom they needed, when at last he heard a voice that sounded like it was being strangled by the cold. A voice asking for Reverend Juan Pablo Almida.

"He cannot come to the phone," Tancredo replied. "Who's calling?" It was the first-ever telephone call to the church asking for Almida at that time of day, and just when Almida was sleeping.

The voice did not identify itself, only asked again for Almida. "He's asleep. Father Almida is sleeping," Tancredo said.

The voice hung up.

"And still asleep," the smallest Lilia added, poking her gray head around the door for an instant, just her head, craning her wrinkled neck, her voice confiding. "Like the sacristan. Will they wake up one day? Who knows? Who can tell? We already gave them their mint tea. They deserved it."

The Lilia's head spoke calmly, in a way that was beyond serene — bored — and every word was perfectly audible; Tancredo even thought he saw her smiling when she asked herself if Almida and Machado would wake up.

The head disappeared abruptly, leaving Tancredo on his own.

Still alone in the sacristy, he observed the arrival of Reverend San José Matamoros with fascination. Wine bottle in hand, the priest's eyes shone as though he were crying.

"I want to sing," he said.

Inebriated, but as if he were being buoyed up by a host of

wings, ebullient, recently showered and shaved, his drunken-ness was betrayed only by his crooked glasses and utterly blank, vacant eyes. He took the cruet from his pocket and showed it to Tancredo triumphantly. "Vodka," he said, and winked. "Father Almida lives like a cardinal." And he belched. Belched, when twenty yards away, at his back, the whole parish was waiting. It was an uncommonly large congregation, judging by the sounds of footsteps, breathing, throat-clearing, coughing. The news of the priest-cantor had spread through the neighborhood like wildfire in the night. The Lilias, Tancredo thought. The Lilias have summoned the whole world.

Then one of them — the small one again — offered him a cup of coffee. The others were helping Matamoros dress, making him splendid in immaculate white and blue. With coffee still on his lips, Tancredo followed behind the priest, passed into the church and was pained by the sight of the altar, with a feeling of regret close to tears. But soon the priest's voice helped him forget, just as the Lilias and all the grandmothers of the Neighbor-hood Civic Association forgot themselves when they heard the sung Our Father, the Blessing, motionless, their hearts as one, their eyes fixed on the little Father, who again retired as if he had just fought the battle of his life. Completely drained, bent dou-ble, Matamoros — as he had done the day before — sat down in the sacristy's only chair, next to the telephone. "One of these days my heart is going to break," he said, and asked Tancredo for a whisky, a whisky, just like that, in the middle of the sac-risty, like being in the bar of one of the brothels Tancredo used to visit in search of diners. Well then: a whisky was conjured up for him, in a tall glass, clinking with ice cubes, immediately, by the three Lilias.

"You are blessed, Father," they said.

In the garden, seated at the edge of the fountain, freckled by the shade of the willow trees, under a cloudless sky and resting on a Friday, that Friday, the first Friday of their lives without cooking, sunk in the tranquil reverie of 11:00 in the morning, the Lilias heard Matamoros singing a bolero, sitting just as they were, beside them, at peace. Nearby, unnoticed by anyone, lurking in corners, leaning against the willows, floating, the seven or nine old ladies of the Neighborhood Civic Association were listening to the sung parable. Tancredo wondered, suddenly discovering that throng of spellbound statues scattered beatifically all around, when exactly the good ladies had entered the presbytery, and had they come through the church? The sacristy? Without asking permission, as if in their own homes? Almost midday, the sun was warming the walls, the time of the Family Meal was approaching, and the Lilias did not go near the kitchen. The adoring old women watched Matamoros drink, heard Matamoros sing, forgetting, or seeming to forget, that Juan Pablo Almida, their parish priest, their benefactor, was asleep and had to be woken up. "I must wake the Father," Tancredo said to himself in one corner of the garden, but remained still, fixated by the song, just as hypnotized as the adoring women, or more so.

"We should wake Father Almida," Sabina said suddenly, beside him, dressed in gray with a gray headscarf, her cold hand lightly touching him. "We have to warn him it's almost midday," she insisted, genuinely startled. "Time for the Family Meal, and Almida and my godfather are still sleeping."

Tancredo did not reply. Sabina's presence froze him, her hand in his.

"But nobody here seems to remember them," Sabina went on. Her marvelling gaze roamed over the women's entranced faces, as if she did not recognize them. "It's unbelievable," she said. "All this for the voice of a drunk." She blushed. "And to think he almost got his talons into me last night." She smiled, transfixed. "It's a miracle in reverse." She was observing Matamoros with the utmost curiosity; did she revere him too? "That Father is on the point of collapse." She was amazed by him. "He's like a party at dawn." And, suddenly anxious: "Nobody seems to realize."

Sabina could stand it no longer. She took a step forward, bit her lip.

"Father Almida won't be long," she yelled at the Lilias, still clutching Tancredo's hand. "Doesn't anybody care?" The song was silenced. Matamoros wiped the sweat from his forehead, rubbed his eyes; was he going to fall asleep? He seemed to sleep whenever it suited him, or had he really sung too much? Whatever the case, the drunken Lilias and the rest of the adoring women froze; time seemed to stand still.

"Father Almida will soon wake up," a Lilia replied evenly. "Friday's his favorite day; he's not going to miss it." Stooping, seated on the edge of the fountain, smiling, almost a girl leaning over the water, she was lit by the rays of the sun. Sabina loathed her.

Then, over and above everything else, came Matamoros's labored voice.

"We can sing the *Te Deum*," he said, his tone sorrowful but self-righteous. "We can repeat Francis Xavier's Act of Contrition, chant a *Trisagion* to the Holy Trinity, offer up devotions to the Sacred Heart, make the Stations of the Cross together: we'll go to the third Station, when Jesus stumbles for the first time, and maybe we'll sing better, or fall asleep; we'll go to the sixth Station, when Veronica wipes His face, and maybe we'll be happy, or unhappy, and unhappier still at the seventh, when Jesus falls for the second time, and at the twelfth we'll die with Jesus dying on the cross, and then, to give thanks for all His suffering, we'll venerate the five Wounds of Christ, we'll sing to the Wound on the left foot, the Wound on the right foot, the Wound on the left hand, the Wound on the right hand, the Wound in His side, and we'll follow on with a prayer to Jesus scourged at the column, Jesus crowned with thorns, and utter the cries of the blessed souls in Purgatory, and then a response, and we will weep for misery."

There was an emphatic silence from the sky.

"Do we want to weep?" the Father asked, getting to his feet. And answered himself immediately: "Never. No more suffering, ever. We don't want to suffer any more."

Just as immediately, he sat down or rather slumped to the ground. He seemed to expire from the effort.

"Rest, Father," the Lilias said, surrounding him.

Only one of the women appeared to take fright at San José's words. Not only did her expression show alarm, her white, wrinkled hand at her brow, but she fainted. There was a commotion of skirts around her. Finally they saw her come to, recover, eyelids fluttering.

"My God," she said, "but I'm fine. The one who needs help is Father San José, bless him."

Faced with this fainting fit and its denouement, Tancredo raised his eyes in resignation. He saw the church's golden dome, ever far off, ever near. And, without intending to, he glanced up at the door of Father Almida's room, on the first floor, which gave onto the garden. The door was open. He could see it was open, from the garden. He immediately headed for the steps, Sabina behind him. They ran up together. It was true: the door was ajar.

They approached on tiptoe. "Father Almida?" The lowered blind created a sort of night, a painful gloom. They leaned over his face. His mouth was set, rigid, twisted, desperate, converted into a silent scream. A slick of green vomit stained the feather pillow.

Sabina ran next door to Machado's room. A few seconds later her scream was heard, short, stifled.

They met in the passage.

It was as if Sabina were levitating, unrecognizable, eyes bright, because, still in the prism of disbelief, she was smiling. Smiling and clasping her hands together. Now she fixed her hope-filled eyes on the sky.

At that point, the Lilias arrived inconveniently. It was as though they were confronting them on the first floor of the presbytery, in the passage green with creepers, in the presence of the other women waiting in the garden. Mute and flushed, the Lilias peered in through the wide-open doors. Then one of their voices could be heard.

"If they don't wake up," she said, as if issuing an order, "we'll have to cry bitterly and pray for the rest of our lives. This is how they arrived from Don Justiniano's house. This is how God brought them back. We didn't even notice, God forgive us. We'll have to cry and pray the rest of our lives."

And they melted away again, down the deep steps.

They reappeared in the garden, arms akimbo, before the group of grandmothers surrounding Reverend San José: he was sleeping like a log. The seven or nine ladies let the Lilias through with a respect bordering on worship. The sun shone, the sky shimmered, but the dark figures crowded around the fountain radiated cold, a portent of rain, a bluish atmosphere, an intimate cloud of ice that obscured the willow trees.

"Take charge," the Lilias told them, "we'll come to you soon, but only when Father Matamoros has rested. Can't you see? He sang too much today."

From the first floor, Tancredo and Sabina were listening. They saw the Lilias take Matamoros away. Were they carrying him again? They could not make him out, hidden amid the old women, their arms open, their black shawls like wings.